THE ADVENT CALENDAR

A collection of short stories

Paula Harmon

Bookcover Artist: Paula Harmon

Also by Paula Harmon:
Murder Britannica
Murder Durnovaria
The Cluttering Discombobulator
Kindling
The Quest
The Seaside Dragon

With Liz Hedgecock
The Caster & Fleet Mysteries

With Val Portelli
Weird and Peculiar Tales

This book is dedicated to my lovely sister Julia with lots of love. (Here's hoping she'll forgive me for fictionalising her in several of these stories.)

Imagine the First of December

You have been given an old fashioned advent calendar.

It contains no chocolate, just twenty-five doors.

Every day in December you open a door and find a picture.

Each one is a picture representing Christmastime.

Now imagine that each of those pictures had a story to tell…

Nativity Play

Despite a yearning to be *Doctor Who*'s assistant which lasted well into adulthood, Angie knew she would never be an actress. It started with her very first Nativity play.

Angie was a realist.

'I'd like to be Mary like you were, Mummy' she said. But she knew it was a vain hope. Her mother was quiet and dark haired. Even if Angie hadn't been mousy brown, she'd already noticed the teacher's attention was caught by the demure girls' capacity to sit in maternal contemplation with the dolls and to do as they were told. She was only five, but somehow Angie realised that her tendency to argue with the teacher when instructions were silly wouldn't get her the demure label.

Still, she didn't really like holding dolls. Looking lovingly at unresponsive plastic faces was not her thing. She was always tempted to cut patterns into their eyelashes and draw on their perfect cheeks. But she would settle for one of the interesting roles. An angel would have been all right. She was after all, on the blonde side of mousy brown and small for her age. She could see herself in the sparkly white and silver, raising her arms, declaiming something dramatic. The teacher couldn't dispute her skill at talking.

Mmm. It turned out chatterboxes didn't get to be angels either. The teacher chose Angie to be the littlest shepherd. She was disgusted. Dressed for a boy's role, in a stripy dressing gown and tea-towel, there was no scope for her to display the femininity lurking under her scabby knees.

She tried hard the following year, but they had decided that only Class One would do the Nativity and Class Two would get to perform a folk tale.

Her mother lovingly made a beautiful Olde Englishe costume: full red skirt, flouncy white blouse, black bodice with laces. She felt beautiful, a princess waiting in disguise for a prince to find her. The only trouble was that instead of coming on to gasps at her beauty, she came on to laughs. The play was something about a pig and the pig was played by the boy from next door crawling resplendent in pink pyjamas. The audience of mothers fell about in stitches.

Class Three: that would be her chance to show the world she could be a star.

The Nativity was still in the sticky hands of Class One. But Angie now felt that being older, they would be able to put on a Christmas play with something like a plot and she would be snapped up for *Doctor Who* in no time. This year however, the school went off piste completely and Angie had to resign herself to being a mother bunny for no reason which she could ever after remember.

Again, her mother lovingly made an outfit, including delightful silky ears. Angie resigned herself to choosing between portraying maternal sentiment or low comedy. Alas, the choice was taken away. When she struck the classic toothy rabbit pose she had to show the world that, just in time for the performance, both her front teeth had fallen out.

That was the point when Angie gave up on a future on the stage.

A couple of years later, her little sister who would have been happy causing mayhem as a shepherd, got to be a Christmas fairy.

Life sucks sometimes.

Holly

It didn't feel like Christmas. The air shimmered with heat and Holly sat under the palms on the beach, perspiring into her sodden dress.

In the market, among piles of fruit and bright clothes, an incongruous two metre inflatable snowman bobbed, poked by boys darting in and out of the shoppers like dusty dragonflies. The vendor, afraid it would burst before it was sold, lashed out in vain as the giggling lads danced away calling out abuse.

In the dry goods store, nodding Santas and reindeers looked exotic between lucky waving cats and genial gods on a shady windowsill. No connection was made with Jesus, portrayed in pictures on temple walls, venerated and worshipped outside of the religion which carried his name but not always his intent.

Holly loved it here. Her colouring meant she was inconspicuous. She lived alone, away from other ex pats and now spoke colloquially, becoming part of the community.

She had arrived leaving behind no-one but her sister Della who had lost her spark to the needle and pill after Dad died. Then, shortly after Holly got the job abroad, Mum died too. She was going to take Della with her, try to help her start again, scatter the ashes in the beautiful tropical ocean. But after the funeral, Della had simply tipped them into the docks and sold the container. When Holly, with teeth gritted, repeated the offer of a new life together abroad, Della's only response had been 'you've got to be kidding but you'll send me money every month right?'

That first Christmas in a new country, Holly had slipped into the tiny church among the temples. No-one noticed her. She was not sure why she was there; perhaps it was a way of honouring the mother whom Della had cast into the cold, diesel smeared sea at home. Within five years she had become just the teacher from somewhere else. And the somewhere else, in her mind was as chill and dull as her sister's eyes had become.

Shortly before the fourth Christmas, an old man and a small girl stopped her in the market.

'He says: telephone your sister,' said the child.

Holly froze. She said, 'tell him: when I left, she didn't even say goodbye. She doesn't answer my texts or anything.'

'He says she needs you.'

The old man, through his gestures, was insistent.

Holly argued, 'she'll have changed her number again.'

The little girl changed tack, 'It'll be snowing where you come from. I wish I could see snow.'

'It won't be,' Holly grimaced, thinking of the grey cold, the dull graffitied walls, the dark underpasses.

'In films…' started the child.

'Films lie,' Holly said, 'if they made a film about here, you would ride on an elephant followed by a tiger.'

The girl giggled, 'that's so silly, there are no elephants or tigers here!'

'Exactly. And it doesn't snow where I come from either. It just rains cold, cold rain.'

The old man interrupted.

'Telephone sister. Go home.'

Over a chilled beer, Holly made the call. There was no answer. Laying her mobile on the scorching table, Holly looked out over the market, its brightness dimmed. She'd give it two more tries.

On the third attempt, someone answered.

'She sold me the mobile,' her old neighbour said, 'needed the cash.'

'Can you get her to ring me?'

For a moment, Holly thought they'd been disconnected. Between them, different seas and continents, religions, customs and regimes spread like spillages on a table cloth. Impossible to imagine words carrying so far.

'Girl...' said the neighbour, 'you'd just best come home.'

Leaving a place where she felt like a butterfly in a cloud of butterflies, Holly constricted herself into shoes and sleeves and boarded a flight that was too long yet over too soon. Stepping out into mid afternoon dusk, into a mass of damp, dark-clad people, she felt like a louse in a nest of squirming lice.

Beyond exuberant Christmas lights and gaudy shop displays, beyond regeneration and gentrification, beyond all but the most apologetic string of coloured bulbs strung across the street, home awaited her. Some kind of winter-dispelling decoration illuminated most windows; but when Holly looked up to the place where she'd grown up, she saw nothing but sheets haphazardly obscuring the glass.

Knocking on the dented door got no response, so she sought the neighbour who had bought her sister's phone.

'Yeah, I gotta key.' said the woman, 'Want me to come along?'

'Thanks.'

'What's it like then, where you live now?' asked the neighbour, between incessant drags from her cigarette, 'dirty innit? Smelly? Stupid hot?'

'Stupid hot for sure,' answered Holly.

'Sort of backward, innit?'

'When did you last see her?' Holly interrupted.

'Coupla weeks maybe,' the neighbour fiddling with the lock, dropped ash on the threshold, 'lots of elephants are there? Do people get ate by tigers much?'

'All the time,' said Holly.

The hallway was dark and bare. New carpets put in six years ago were gone. In the little kitchen, half opened packets spewed their contents, but there was no fridge, no kettle, no microwave. A cracked bar of budget soap had dried out in the bathroom; the bedrooms were bare of all but dusty floorboards. Holly tried to convince herself that the place was empty but she knew it wasn't. As she took a deep breath and pushed open the sitting room door, she heard a mew, like a cat. But there was no smell of cat.

On old stained sheets on the floor, lay Della. Holly would never have recognised her. She traced her own cheekbones as she knelt down to touch the skeletal face. Was this what lay beneath her own skin? Her sister opened paper thin eyelids and peered up. A scrawny hand pulled down the sheet a little and the mewing sound increased. Against clothes stained with leaking milk, a tiny baby balled its hands and puckered its mouth like a goldfish.

Holly turned to the neighbour, 'Didn't you know…'

'Well sorta. Wasn't really sure, she's that thin.'

Holly lifted the baby out. Bundled in a tee-shirt, it was too weak to cry. Would she have to expose her Della's breast? How did you get a baby to latch on?

'Don't you have a go at me,' argued the neighbour into Holly's silence, taking another drag, 'where was you when she got this bad? Out on your tropical island or wherever. She's not *my* problem?'

'I left because she never cared about me. She didn't care about anything.'

'So what do *you* care about, your majesty?'

'Give me a hand, can't you?' snapped Holly. The neighbour ground her cigarette butt into the floor and lit another, holding it between her lips as she helped sit Della up.

'Bottles are better,' she mumbled through the cigarette, 'it's not like we're cows.'

With one hand, Holly dialled 999.

'They'll get the social involved,' warned the neighbour.

'Who's the father?' mouthed Holly.

The neighbour rolled her eyes.

At the hospital, they said there was nothing they could do for Holly's sister but against the odds, the baby would survive.

Holly held Della's dry hand. She avoided the cannula which was dripping pain relief to ease these last hours. Her knee bumped against the catheter bag. Meaningless bleeps monitored her sister's progress from one world to another.

'Has he got a name, Della?' she asked. There was no response. After a pause she said, 'You should have come with me. It would have been... Do you want to know what it's like? It's lovely out there. The sun shines all year round. I love it. There's such a sense of community, family....'

She dried up and felt blood rush to her face. Her sister's eyes opened and focussed on her for a second.

'Della?'

Her sister's lips moved but nothing could be heard.

'Keep talking?' she guessed.

The tiniest nod.

'I'm sorry... I was so angry...' she started.

The tiniest shake of the head. A squeeze of the hand.

'Your life...' a breath.

'You want to hear more?'

Nod.

'It's too hot to move but everyone's on the move all the time anyway. It's so bright, so many colours, it's like Christmas every day. The people are so...'

'Still angry?' whispered Della.

Holly sat still and looked into those eyes. Somehow, her mind overlaid them, in those last moments with the happy, funny eyes from long long ago. Was she still angry?

'No. It doesn't matter anymore.'

'Baby?'

'Social services will find a good family for him.'

'All alone.'

'He'll be fine. Don't worry. I'll make sure of it.'

'Promise?'

Holly nodded. Were the bleeps slowing, the lines flattening?

'Elephants? Tigers?' whispered her Della.

Holly swallowed, 'everywhere,' she said, 'some of the kids come to school on elephants and we need high fences to keep the tigers out.'

The tiniest conspiratorial grin, whispering: 'I wish…'

The eyelids closed.

The nurse came and adjusted some dials.

She murmured, 'We don't need the monitors anymore love, just keep holding her hand, just keep talking. It won't be long now.'

Under the palm, Holly found it hard to believe another year had passed. On her eventual return, she had searched for the old man and his grand-daughter but failed. She wanted to thank him, to ask him how he knew. But in a place of family and community, her descriptions matched no-one. All the same, she had brought back a snow globe just in case, one day, she could hand it over to the little girl who didn't have a tiger and introduce her to a little boy who had no mother but had an aunt who, in the end, could not bear to leave him behind.

Train Set

They say that travel broadens the mind but all it had done for Laura's mind was fill it with glue.

She'd always thought offices were pretty lethal but after a while you become immune to your colleagues. Commuting was something else on the germ warfare front.

It was the festive season and therefore also the cold season. Taking the 7:47 train to London yet again, Laura felt more at risk of pleurisy than terrorism. The coughing and sneezing had started before they'd left the station. Unseen beyond the seat back, a young man made a noise which sounded like a particularly wet explosion. Laura was already headachy and slightly nauseous. She daren't look, she daren't look. The young man's girlfriend was laughing because he hadn't got a tissue.

"There's snot everywhere! It's all over your face and dripping off your hands!' she guffawed.

Laura wanted to throw up, but let's be honest, however silently you do it, vomiting is frowned on in the silent carriage. She wondered if it was possible to hold your breath from Salisbury to Waterloo and concluded that it wouldn't help, the germs were probably burrowing in through her very skin. They would probably then have a party with the ones already filling her lungs with porridge.

Averting her eyes as the young man went to find some loo roll to clean himself up, Laura's respiratory system decided to protest and she started to cough herself, remembering that she'd left the box of tissues on the ironing board and now had a total of two to see her through an hour and a half. Laura sat back. She felt hungover, or rather, slightly drunk, in that out of focus, time lapse way where you never wanted to drink again. Sitting in a meeting all day was going to be fun.

At Waterloo, it seemed that the whole world was shuffling for the tube. A zombie invasion couldn't have looked much different: more groaning perhaps and less takeaway coffee. Looking down into the abyss which led to the Jubilee line, Laura was mesmerised by the blurry escalator taunting her lack of balance. More coughing and sneezing in the tube and worse, it was so crowded she was held up purely by the passengers around her. Unable to grab a hand hold, her face pressed was against a stranger's winter clad chest as she tried not to pierce his foot with her heels when they stopped. She didn't normally stand this close to people she actually liked.

At London Bridge she emerged and headed for the Thames. She was aware that the wind was bitter but an internal flame was making her feel unpleasantly clammy inside her winter coat. It had been a long time since breakfast. She rushed along for a while, caught up in the weft going east, which was weaving an intricate pattern through the western bound warp of tourists and day trippers, from time to time knotting up in tangles of unantici-pated human contact and apologies.

Coming to the river, Laura unpicked herself from the for-ward motion and went to peer over the wall and down onto the sludgy waters of the Thames. It looked pretty much how she imagined the contents of her lungs, only more fluid. And possibly healthier. Turning back, bracing herself to plunge back into the fray, she wondered what the point was. Where was everyone go-ing and why? What would happen if they all stopped and went for coffee instead? For that matter what would happen if *she* went for coffee instead?

Well she was early enough to sit in a coffee house for a bit. She sat at a table in a corner, obscured by a Christmas tree, her eyes ringing with seasonal pop music and let the world drift out of focus.

'I can't believe she's wearing that suit.'

Laura opened her eyes. For a moment, she wondered where she was, and why she was lying on a row of chairs behind a sticky table. She wondered how she could sit up without anyone notic-ing. Then she realised there were two women sitting opposite her. Not only did they look familiar but they were scrutinising her.

'I can't believe she's drinking that coffee.'

'What's wrong with it?'

'It's not organic. Or free-trade. I always said I'd never drink anything else.'

'Did we?'

Laura sat up and shook her head.

'You look like you feel like death,' said one of the women. Her clothes were unique. Pretty but not expensive. Laura had never seen them on the high street. The woman's hair was short and neat, her face was un-made up. She had an air of utter calm.

'If you'd stuck to the organic, free-trade food like you said you would, you'd be healthier. I bet you eat ready meals and everything,' said the other woman. Her clothes were also odd, but in a different sort of way. She looked as if she'd raided a number of charity shops for the most clashing items she could find. Her curly hair was long and chaotic and her make-up was vibrant.

Laura, in her grey trouser suit with her shoulder hair straightened and her make up discrete, felt drab as well as sick. What strengthened this feeling was the fact that the other two women were herself. It was like looking into one of those online tools to experiment with hairstyles.

She closed her eyes. They'd go away if she closed her eyes.

The calm one poked her arm. 'Wake up, we've only got half an hour. Mind you that coffee's gone cold, want some more?'

'Make sure it's organic,' called out the chaotic one, and then, 'Really, we've only got half an hour. Which one do you wish you were?'

'What?' said Laura, opening her eyes.

'Don't you remember coming here twenty years ago?'

Laura looked round. It was just another chain coffee shop. She shrugged.

'You must remember. It wasn't generic then, it was independent. We, you, I had just had a job interview and been offered the job. It was decision time. Now it's winter solstice and it's decision time again. Our universes are touching. Each of us is the you that took one of the paths on offer twenty years ago. We could swap worlds if we want.'

Laura groaned. The fever was worse than she'd thought.

The calm one came back and put a cup of coffee in front of her. The chaotic one said to the calm one:

'Who are you? I don't remember the option to be you!'

'I went to work for a charity in a developing country. I'm still there. I don't suppose you remember me because you considered the possibility for all of ten seconds.'

Laura frowned. Oh yes, now she recalled it. The options on the table: work her way up the corporate ladder, take a risk on her creative skills or save the world. In the end, she'd looked back on her childhood with parents wondering how to pay the bills and crossed the charity work off almost immediately. It wasn't just the money, it was the isolation, the possibility she'd never meet anyone to replace the boy she'd be leaving behind. Maybe never have children…

'Are you married?' she asked.

The calm one shook her head.

'Do you mind?'

'It's just the way it is. I have a different sort of family, a different role in the community. But I wake up every day eager to get back to work. I can't imagine retiring.'

'What about you?' Laura asked the chaotic one who looked down at the table.

Oh yes, the second option. Be a potter. Be organic. Make everything from scratch from your own garden. Give up meat maybe. Don't let avarice mar the creative spark. Be poor. Marry the boy without whom Laura's world had been meaningless for five endless years.

'You married him didn't you?'

The chaotic one nodded but didn't look up immediately.

'It didn't work out. You were right, it was a mistake.'

'Any children?' Laura imagined them as she had imagined them all those years ago. The four children she and the boy would have together. She could see their faces, their hair, an amalgamation of their parents. Once their imagined faces had taunted her for a long time after she had given up hope of their existence.

'No. Or at least, not with him. I married again afterwards. Now I've got four with my second husband. And you?'

Laura sighed.

'Married with a daughter. Thought it would never happen for a long time. Then it did. She's lovely. How about the pottery?'

The chaotic one laughed and pulled a wry face, 'we manage. Just about. The vegetarian make-it-from-scratch option is pretty much an economic necessity. But... truth is, I wake up every day and can't wait to get started on the clay.'

'What about you, Laura?' asked the calm one. 'Is that how you feel about *your* job?'

'It has its moments,' said Laura, 'but mostly it pays the bills and gives us a bit of security.'

She started to cough, observing through running eyes, the two other Lauras who exuded the hopes, potential and aspirations of twenty years ago. What had she missed?

'I've just joined an art group,' she said when she could speak again, 'We're building a workshop in the garden for me. I've worked part-time since my daughter was born and now she's at school, I'm going to start being creative again. I can't pretend that otherwise I'm like either of you.'

'I think the point is,' said the calm one, 'are we content with who we are?'

Without a pause, all three said 'Yes' and Laura sneezed.

When she opened her eyes she was alone.

She shook her head and looked at her watch. It was nearly time to go. Or should she just take the train home again? No-one was going to want to sit in a meeting room with her coughing and sneezing for five hours.

As she left, she bumped into a colleague rushing in the direction of the office.

'Oh dear,' said the colleague, stopping to look into Laura's face, 'you really don't look like you feel yourself at all.'

'Funnily enough,' Laura answered, 'I feel completely myself. But I'm going home anyway.'

Christmas Trees

Once, a long time ago, the little girl had gone to sleep in her warm cosy bed next to her brother in his warm cosy bed.

That night the bomb fell. She woke to a mouth full of dust and ears full of screams and saw her brother's arm poking out lifeless from under rubble. After that, her mother and father took her on a long journey away from the bad men.

They travelled by truck and then by boat churning in the inky black sea and then on foot for miles and miles. Her mother tried to make it fun, tried to make it seem like an adventure but the road was long and hard and with each step they were leaving behind her brother. When she closed her eyes, she still saw his arm sticking out of the rubble as if it was sticking out from under the covers, as if in a minute he would wake up and they could start playing.

They thought they had left the bad men, but not everyone they met was friendly, neither the men in the truck nor the men on the boat, nor some of the people they passed on their long walk. It is not just bombs that wound. Every night, the little girl tried to stay awake as long as she could because she was afraid of waking up to dust and screams. Every night, her mother said 'not many more days'. She had been saying that for a long time.

When they had started it was summer. The days were hot and the nights warm. Now it was winter and they were in a strange land. The houses looked different and the trees did too. Some of the trees looked like Christmas trees.

The little girl's family didn't celebrate Christmas but they had seen the movies and the merchandise and the hype and she knew a Christmas tree when she saw one. Now the days were cold and the nights colder. They had little to sleep on, some cardboard and some blankets. Her parents tried to keep her warm as she lay awake under the Christmas trees, wondering if they would walk forever and ever and ever; whether it would get colder and colder.

She looked up through the branches of the Christmas tree and thought of the movies and the merchandise. Families gathered round trees, in warm, bright houses not in frozen, dark woods. They laughed at the cold, they didn't huddle miserably in it. The snow in movies looked fun and exciting not just one more layer of bitter chill. And whatever happened, whatever problems the people faced, in the end Christmas, whatever it was supposed to be, came and everyone opened their presents and were happy.

The little girl watched as a few snowflakes made it through the branches and landed on her face. She thought of herself and her parents and the others. She imagined them as presents lying under the tree, waiting to be found, waiting to be wanted on Christmas Day.

She hoped Christmas would come soon and find them.

Father Christmas

Father Christmas had a headache.

It is quite bad enough waking up after eleven months' serious snoozing and getting yourself in shape for the most frenetic twenty-hours known to mythic kind, without being pestered by someone with a daft idea before you've built up the strength to argue.

On 1st December it had been Bob from Elf and Safety, checking out the sleigh's seat belt and luggage restraint system.

'Don't forget, an object will remain at rest or in uniform motion in a straight line unless acted upon by an external force. How fast will you be travelling again?'

'10,703,437.5 km/hr, whatever that is in old money.'

'Well, you don't want to be slapped in the back of the head with your sack if you have to do an emergency stop do you?'

'Indeed I don't,' Father Christmas replied, his mind boggling.

On 2nd December, when Father Christmas was still waiting for his third cup of coffee to kick in, Eric the Green turned up to do an emissions test on the reindeer.

'Their emissions are waaaaay above the advertised levels!' he exclaimed.

'It's the sprouts,' said Father Christmas glumly, 'I keep trying to stop them from eating them, but the pixies sneak them in when I'm not looking.'

On 3rd December, an Elficiency Consultant called Harry appeared. He was sporting a stop watch, a lot of multi-coloured post-it notes and a great deal of flip chart paper.

'We need to get your team working in a more modern way,' Harry announced.

'Why?' asked Father Christmas, 'It's been working fine this way since 1840.'

'You gotta continually improve the service you give your customers so they are delighted rather than enraged.' Harry explained.

'That's not generally a problem,' argued Father Christmas in bafflement, 'unless the parents give me a duff set of instructions or the child is a spoilt brat.'

'Nah, see, I've been gemba-ing...'

'Is that a new dance craze?'

'No, look listen, "gemba" means "go see". I've been to see how everyone does things to see if there's a more organised way to work.'

'Everyone who?'

'Tooth fairy: could she swap the teeth for money quicker? Cupid: is there a more reliable means of ensuring the right people get stuck with the arrow? Fairy Godmother: could she plan ahead a bit more and avoid the unnecessary torment of pumpkins?'

'And could they?'

'No, they were pretty efficient, truth be told. I did the lead in time and a value stream map and they seemed to have their jobs down to a fine art.'

Although Father Christmas had no idea what Harry was on about, he wasn't surprised about the efficiency, he couldn't imagine any of those three wasting unnecessary time working when they could be sitting round a toadstool drinking mead and putting both the mythic and human world to rights.

'Mind they're all self employed - now you - you've got a team and what is there *not* in team?'

'Nonsense?'

'No, 'I'.' Harry sensed a bafflement in his listener's face, 'There's no 'i' in team.'

'Well no, it's spelled...'

'So, anyway, what I'm going to do is do some time and motion with your guys, check out their success register and their concerns log and come back tomorrow and do some creative problem solving.'

Father Christmas watched Harry bounce off into the work-shop brandishing his stop watch and wondered if it was actually still November and he was actually still asleep and having a nightmare.

On 4th December, Father Christmas was just tucking into his third cooked breakfast when he was simultaneously visited by someone from Gladys from Elf and Wellbeing and Malc from Manelfment.

Gladys tutted at the black pudding and the builder's tea with three sugars.

'What kind of example are you setting to your staff?' she exclaimed, 'At least you're not drinking that beverage they gave you sponsorship for. That's got even more sugar in.'

'I might be driven to something stronger in a minute,' argued Father Christmas, 'I've got an image to maintain. I've been asleep for eleven months, I've got some serious work to do on my figure. Look! My belt's all loose!'

Malc was more concerned about performance targets and job descriptions and started brandishing a lot of spreadsheets arguing about increasing production by reducing the elf-force.

At this point Harry returned, trying to smile bravely while announcing that the workshop could not be more efficient if it tried.

Father Christmas exploded.

'I don't know what you've been doing while I've been asleep but it sounds like you've all spent far too much time in the human world getting your knickers in a twist dabbling in things humans make up because they seem to think life isn't complicated enough already. Let me make this clear to you all because you've clearly forgotten: everything we do is done by magic. Everything. The Tooth Fairy, the Fairy Godmother, Cupid, me. The elves get all the presents ready by magic; the sleigh and reindeer fly by magic; I get round the entire world in twenty four hours by magic; I get down chimneys by magic. I can eat what I want because I'm magic and I've been around for thousands of years in one form or another and one more bit of bacon isn't going to make a differ-ence now. Now get rid of your stop watches and bits of paper and go and do something important. Go and make a present for a child who maybe has something real to worry about and could do with a boost.'

The three elves looked a little crestfallen. It had seemed such a good idea. Humans seemed to like it. Harry tentatively tried one last time:

'Er - Father Christmas, I really want to try the creative prob-lem solving. It looks like fun. Have you really got no problems I could try it out on?'

Father Christmas filled his lungs ready to roar and then de-flated them again.

'Actually, now I come to think of it,' he said, 'I've got one. It's that fashion for log burners. I mean I can get down a chimney by magic, and children with no chimneys leave me those magic keys. But those log burners fox me every time. I keep getting stuck inside and last year Mrs Christmas was really annoyed about all the scorched pants.'

He sighed and rolled his eyes as Harry merrily started get-ting his post-it notes out. Oh well, anything for a quiet life.

Presents

When the Martian invasion took place, we thought we were doomed to slavery or annihilation; but it turned out the Martians had simply been watching us for centuries and when we got to the brink of self destruction, decided they had to help.

They started by tackling inequalities. Anyone who had achieved power by virtue of gender or wealth or family was sent off to Mars for re-education and kept until they felt able to change their views. Unsurprisingly to us, but surprising to the Martians, very few came back. No-one was too sorry about this to start with, because let's face it, the people left behind were mostly those who'd suffered the inequality.

The first Christmas after the invasion, the Martians decided it was the perfect opportunity to work with humans on recognising what is important.

'Isn't this festival about someone who came to teach about weakness conquering strength, light conquering darkness, about forgiveness, neighbourliness, new beginnings?' they said.

Most people said 'no - it's about presents.'

So the Martians invited all adults to a present-giving. Life was a little dull now that excessive wealth was discouraged, so this was exciting.

On arrival, we were each given a token and then sent alone into a room with two machines. The instructions said something like this:

Machine One: Use your token here if you wish to receive a gift whose value is slightly greater than your material wealth. E.g. if you are on a lower than average income, you will get a physical gift which is slightly higher than average value and so on. You can keep this gift or sell it as you wish. There is no guarantee that receiving this gift will make you happy; in fact research suggests that the more people possess beyond essentials, the less content they are.

Machine Two: Use your token here if you wish to receive a gift which is unrelated to economic status. It will not be a physical gift but a spiritual one. It might be the gift of love or forgiveness or kindness or faith or peace-making or generosity or comforting. There is no guarantee that receiving a gift like this will make you happy but research suggests that it is likely to make you more content and of greater value to your fellow human being.

I probably don't need to tell you which machine received the most tokens. And perhaps you're also not surprised to hear that most people who received a gift from Machine One complained bitterly: it wasn't what they wanted, it wasn't valuable enough, etc etc …

The Martians wearily tackled all the subsequent disputes and noticed that people who had once complained about inequality were now trying to get wealthy and powerful at the expense of their fellows.

'It's like you all have an incurable disease,' they said, giving up and returning to Mars.

I wish they'd left Machine Two. God knows we need it. Perhaps another time, we'd have the sense to use it.

Turkey

Even after Bill died, Janie was invited to his great nephew Derek's house for Christmas Dinner in the name of tradition.

She was fairly certain they didn't really want her. They wanted Bill, with his daft sense of humour, his nonstop banter, his delight over cracker jokes, the silly faces he played for the kids, the way he tucked into all the food with gusto. Never too many turkey leftovers to worry about when Bill had been around. Janie felt like the boring relation in the corner. She wasn't good at telling jokes and years of never getting a word in edgeways meant that she didn't always have much to say for herself. Children in general didn't really interest her, but she was fond of Derek's, especially when they'd been small. Now they were a bit too old to lean against her and listen to stories, or look at the pictures she'd taken. Since she'd taken up digital photography, Derek's lad would sometimes help her with a tricky bit of editing; but mostly the kids spent Christmas day in their bedrooms glued to various devices, on line to friends in other bedrooms somewhere else entirely.

Meanwhile, Derek and his wife, having loaded the dishwasher, put on the TV, poured more wine and, having run out of things to say to Janie, always fell asleep. Janie was left to herself, manipulating photographs or reading.

Every year, Janie wondered why she'd come. She could be sitting at home with a simple meal, something on the TV she actually wanted to watch at the right volume. But then she'd be all on her own at Christmas, like Mr Baxter next door.

'Poor old chap,' Derek's wife would say, 'fancy not having anywhere to go at Christmas.'

Bill had once suggested that they invite him round, but Derek's wife said she couldn't really afford to buy the extra food and anyway, Christmas was a family thing, and he was bound to have nephews or nieces or what have you. He become a bit of a curmudgeon since his wife died, so maybe he preferred it, maybe he was a bit of a Bah Humbug type.

When Bill had been alive, he and Janie used to drive to Derek's house and park up, getting out with their presents and their contributory bottle of wine and wave at Mr Baxter who appeared to be looking out of the window to make sure they weren't blocking his drive with their car. He would raise his hand in salute and withdraw. A man in his early seventies, a little stooped, one of those faces you couldn't read.

Janie had long since lost her confidence for driving, so the Christmas after Bill died, Derek picked her up from the station. Since there was no risk of Mr Baxter's drive being blocked she had assumed he wouldn't come to the window, but there he was, watching as she struggled unassisted out of Derek's car and raising his hand in salute as usual. When she went home in a taxi (since Derek was over the limit) Mr Baxter must have spotted her leaving because he came out to shake her hand. He simply said 'sorry to hear about your husband. You feel sort of adrift don't you?' and when she couldn't think of anything to say except yes, her throat constricting, he withdrew back into his house.

The following two Christmases, he saluted her again and when Derek wasn't looking made the gesture for 'do you fancy a drink?' and smiled encouragingly. Janie smiled back but pointing towards Derek, shook her head.

This year, he smiled from his window and saluted and raised his eyebrows slightly. This time, Janie didn't shake her head, she waggled her hand: maybe.

Present opening was over quickly. It didn't take long for Derek's family to open the envelopes of cash which they'd requested or for her to unwrap a teaset. It was very pretty teaset, but she wasn't entirely sure why they thought she needed one after fifty years of marriage and inheriting china from two sets of parents.

Derek and his wife served up a delicious meal as usual and once the dishwasher was loaded and the children had sloped off to their rooms, fell asleep in front of some soap opera on the television.

Janie sat for a while and contemplated whether to try and wrest the remote control out of Derek's grip. She felt as lonely here as she would have if she'd been at home on her own. As if she'd been Mr Baxter. Then she quietly packed up her laptop and her coat and tiptoed out of the house, closing the door behind her.

On Derek's front doorstep, she drew in a deep breath of the cold damp December air and admiring the effect of the dimming afternoon light on the lamp-posts and shrubbery of the suburban street, took a quick photograph with the camera she carried everywhere with her.

Mr Baxter opened his front door on the second ring. He didn't express much surprise but he grinned. It was a cheeky grin full of warmth and delight. He ushered her in to the hall, its walls festooned with photographs and modern art and then into his sitting room, decorated in old gold and wine red for Christmas.

'Soft drink, tea or sherry?' he said, taking her coat, 'or I've a bottle of prosecco I've been keeping by.'

'Keeping for what?' asked Janie.

'For when you changed your mind,' said Mr Baxter.

'Best open it then,' said Janie.

Derek woke up with a snort a couple of hours later and looking around realised something was missing. For a while, he couldn't work out what it was and then he saw the empty chair in the corner. They couldn't fathom about where Aunt Janie had gone and in the end he went out onto the street to see if she was wandering about. She hadn't seemed to have got to that stage but you never knew.

Mr Baxter's lights were on and he hadn't drawn the curtains. Perhaps he'd seen her. Derek walked up the path and looked into the sitting room. There were Mr Baxter and Great Aunt Janie playing a board game and laughing. He felt hurt: wasn't their company good enough? Christmas was for family wasn't it? Then he thought about what sort of company they offered his great aunt and felt ashamed.

He tapped on the window and beckoned them outside.

Janie came to the door, her mouth set and her shoulders dropped: 'is the taxi coming soon?' she asked.

'No,' said Derek, 'I haven't ordered one. I've been thinking Aunt Janie - you can have Amy's bed - stay over. Come back and have some port and cake. We'll drag the kids out their rooms and play a game of something. Come on - both of you - let's make this a Christmas to remember.'

Fairy

The invisible household elves were socially embarrassed. Their humans, always a little behind, hadn't decorated at all.

'Even the house at the top of the hill has its lights on,' complained Peaseblossom, 'why do we have to live in such with such a disorganised family?'

'Well, the place needs tidying first. Where are they going to put it all at the moment?' pointed out Harebell reasonably, 'I mean school bags, shoes, DIY stuff, briefcases, books everywhere. I don't know why she doesn't just put glitter on the cobwebs and have done with it.'

'Do what to me?' asked Cobweb who had her head in a novel as usual and wasn't paying attention.

'Not you - them' Peaseblossom said, pointing at the webs wafting in the draft in the corners.

'Pity you can't get Brownies anymore.' sighed Harebell nostalgically.

Cobweb opened her mouth.

'Not chocolate brownies - Brownies who do the housework. They were never the same after they got feminism and burnt their brooms. Bless her, she could do with a Brownie.'

'We could help,' suggested Puck, 'she always liked the "Elves and the Shoemaker" when she was little.'

'Stuff that for a game of soldiers,' snorted Peaseblossom, 'anyway, what's she doing?'

Their female human was rooting through a dusty, slightly dented cardboard box. She was pulling things out at random and exclaiming; black and white photographs, a Peter and Jane book with the title characters clasping their gender specific toys (doll or train set) or helping with gender specific activities (washing up or making things). It was perhaps no surprise that this woman had rejected the hallowed role of housewife at the earliest opportunity in exchange for something more interesting. First she'd found some very faded bits of paper and was trying to make chains with them. Then she'd found a flat piece of yellow card which, once she'd fiddled with it for a while, turned into a three dimensional dust-catcher in the shape of a bell.

'The things humans find exciting,' said Puck, shaking his head.

'Don't be mean,' argued Harebell, 'she found it in the stuff her Mum couldn't take to her new flat. It's a box of memories. Oh good grief, look what she's dug out now.'

It was a celluloid fairy; a stiff net sequinned skirt, once pink, wired net wings, a tiny silver wand clasped in her plastic hand, an insipid pouting face and blonde curls. The human got up from her kneeling position and started jumping up and down.

'That's got to date back to before she was even born, 1962 looking at those clothes. Real fairies don't dress like that any-more!' snorted Puck disgustedly. The others ignored him, yearn-ing for a more romantic age, although admittedly a sequinned net skirt looked a bit scratchy.

Their male human had come to see what the fuss was about and was looking as baffled as his invisible watchers felt to see his wife waving an old grubby plastic fairy as if it was the holy grail.

'It was what Mum put on our tree what I was really little!' she was telling him, 'we could use it this year instead of that con-stipated looking angel.'

Puck, Peaseblossom and Harebell looked on in disbelief. It's not as if the decorations in their house were ever sophisticat-ed, but at least they were relatively contemporary give or take a couple of decades.

'Just as well that fairy isn't real' said Cobweb without look-ing up from her novel. 'I think the tinsel's come off the top of their fake tree - just a spike left. She'd soon wipe that sickly smile off her face when she realised what she's got to sit on.'

Sheep

After his baby girl died before they even got her home from hospital, Rob gave everything up.

Not quite everything. He gave up his good job, his expensive car and big house but he kept his wife and his young son and together they moved onto a small holding in the middle of nowhere.

Rob would have been the first to admit he knew next to nothing about farming, but having to learn something from scratch, having to fight the earth and the weather and the chickens and drag something like a living out of it made some sort of sense, when nothing else did. The hard work made him sleep, the set backs and the trials were like a punishment; the penalty for being alive when Lucy was dead.

The years went by and he learned and the small holding started to work. They would never be rich, but nothing they could buy would now be worth the same as a lost child. When someone asked about whether his wife had minded, he said that she had hated her job anyway and now she was crafting all day and selling things she'd made with pride, although they rarely fetched much more than the cost of materials. Once, when she was ill, he overheard someone at the school gate talking about her charity shop clothes. He briefly realised that perhaps he ought to encourage her to buy some new stuff, but he forgot it by the time he got home. When someone asked if his son minded, he said it was good for the boy to learn about real things like life and death and hard work, rather than sitting at a computer all day. He was proud of his wife and son, but he never remembered to tell them. He was not good with words.

His son grew older. In his early teens he had brought a girl home from school to help out. 'Just a friend' he said. Now he was nearly eighteen and she was still coming round to help, clearly more than a friend, his son smiling like the sun when she was there.

This winter, Rob had decided to branch out. They needed a bit more cash and he had bought some lambs to fatten up and sell in spring. Lambs! They were enormous, yearlings. Rob knew nothing much about sheep and disliked them. He didn't like their smell, their stupidity, the grease in their wool, their dirty rear ends, the way they looked impassively at him - scared, happy, excited - who could tell? He took the seller's word for it that they were fine and there was nothing he need do except feed them and keep them safe.

It was a bitter night when his son came into the house and called for him. They had herded the sheep into a barn for the duration of the cold snap and the girlfriend was there, helping out again. Her father had sheep and she was comfortable with them.

'Dad! Dad! Come quick - there's a baby lamb!'

Rob didn't believe him, 'can't be - the males are all castrated - the females were all checked - that's what he said.'

'Honest Dad - come and see!'

Out in the barn the sheep were milling about being smelly and noisy. In amongst them all, a tiny lamb was staggering to its feet, about to be trampled, its mother nosing it towards her udder. A moment later, the girlfriend called out: 'here's another one!'

Rob watched as his son's girlfriend waded in among the sheep, separating the labouring mothers, showing his son how to help with the births until they were a team, their hands smeared with blood. Each tiny lamb struggled to start with but when one was born unmoving, the two young people worked together until it drew breath. Rob saw them catching each other's eyes and smiling, lost in their own world of love and pride. That was how he felt about his wife, but when was the last time he had looked at her like that, had looked at her at all?

He left them to it and went inside. His wife was in the sitting room, working at her crafts and watching TV. She was older, but she was still lovely, patient, supportive and for the first time, he had room to acknowledge that she must be carrying her own grief too. She looked up and he saw that her eyes were full of tears. On the TV there was an appeal for children's clothes and blankets for those hundreds of children caught up in wars and trekking with crowds of refugees, innocent of all except being born in the wrong country at the wrong time - about to start freezing in their camps.

Rob said nothing but went up into the wardrobe and came back down with the box of brand new clothes they'd put together for Amy but which she'd never worn. He put it down in front of his wife and he put his arms round her and they wept. He was not good with words, but his wife knew what he was trying to say.

They opened the box for the first time in ten years, lifting out each item - the babygrows, the pretty dresses and the soft woollen blankets and the little toy lamb they thought she could cuddle one day. They were all immaculate, untarnished; just waiting for someone who needed them.

And now it was finally time to let them go.

Carol-Singers

By the time our parents let us out to go carol-singing it was too late. Lee Price and his gang had been up and down the street and stripped it bare.

It wasn't quite so much the loss of pickings, it was more the fact they put no effort into it and we did.

Take Guy Fawkes Night for example. Now, where we lived when I was young, we didn't do trick or treating. I'm not sure we'd even heard of it. The most mischief anyone got up to at Hallowe'en was to make a Jack O'Lantern and stick it on someone's front wall to glare into their house but Guy Fawkes' night was another matter. In the general build up to the bonfire and fireworks, the few children of our small village would make an effigy out of whatever was to hand and would cart it from house to house demanding 'a penny for the guy'.

In that particular November, Ffion and I, with some inadequate help from our little sisters, had made an elaborate guy from various cast-offs. Ffion's mother, in secret triumph, had contributed some despised trousers which Ffion's father wore to go rabbiting. Over a newspaper body, the guy wore a holey jumper of my dad's which had been darned in odds and ends of wool into a puckered patchwork. But Ffion and I were mostly proud of the effigy's head. We had made it from a papier-mâché covered balloon so that it was actually head-shaped. We had drawn a life-like face and sacrificed some of our little sisters' dolls' hair to make a moustache and beard, and found an old hat at the back of a wardrobe to cover his baldness.

Carrying him off in triumph we did our rounds of the houses up our street; only the Price boys had been round earlier and got most of the money and all the laughs by dressing Rhys up as a guy and wheeling him round in an old pushchair.

Thing was, our village was small and not especially wealthy. Generosity of spirit, of which there was plenty, doesn't buy you sweets. You had to get in first.

Ready for carol-singing, Ffion and I had, once again, perfected our image. No-one was going to buy us the Dickensian outfits my femininity yearned for (which, looking back, was probably a relief to the jeans-clad others); but we wore our best clothes and had practiced our carols till we were pitch and word perfect. We had even made lanterns out of glittery paper-decorated jam jars. There were night-lights inside and we'd devised a complicated carrying arrangement that stopped our hands from being burnt and which we hoped would not somehow ignite as we made our way up and down the cold drizzly street.

Trouble was, before we were allowed out, we had to have dinner and assure our parents we were safe etcetera etcetera. Dad had insisted I take something warming for us to drink which meant I had to carry an awkward glass bottle in my school satchel as well as everything else. Meanwhile, the Price boys, whose parents didn't care what they did, were out singing a mixture of carols (the school-yard versions) and rugby songs and were raking in the cash.

We hit the street just as everyone was settling down in front of the TV and didn't feel like opening the door to four earnest little girls and a blast of chilly damp air.

By the time we'd got to the little low cottage at the end of the road, our money bag felt not much heavier than when we started. It was too dark to see what we'd got, but we were pretty sure the effort hadn't been worth it.

We knew Mrs Morgan was in, because the downstairs lights were all on. We sang our way through 'The First Nowell' and knocked on the door but she didn't come out. After some consultation, we knocked on the door again and started 'Angels from the Realms of Glory' because we were quite proud at how long we could sing 'Gloooooooria' before we had to take a breath.

Mrs Morgan opened the door a crack and peered out.

'Oh, it's you lot,' she said, 'I thought it might be them Price boys again.'

We swallowed the affront that our singing could in any way be compared and smiled the smiles of sweet innocent girlhood.

'I'm not sure I got any change, mind,' she apologised, 'but I got mince pies and welshcakes.'

I could sense Ffion's shoulders sag but our sisters were undaunted.

'Both please!' they cried to our shame.

Mrs Morgan grinned and looked at us a bit more closely as we stood there in a pool of light from the hall, our hair sparkling with drizzle, our faces red from the cold. She bit her lip and peered over her shoulder. Then she said, 'oh come on in girls, I can't have you freezing on the doorstep.'

Raising her eyebrows at our 'lanterns', Mrs Morgan made us blow out the night-lights and leave them outside in the rain. We hung our dripping coats on hooks by the door and left our shoes to drain into the mat.

Settling us in the sitting room she went to make us some cocoa.

'No touching anything mind,' she instructed, 'and keep away from the hearth.'

The sitting room was festooned with paper chains in dull pinks and reds and greens. They looped from corner to corner and across the mirror on the chimney breast where they swayed in the heat of the fire. A very small white tinsel Christmas Tree covered in fairy lights and glass baubles stood in front of the window. Around us, there was barely room for a few dark side tables, covered in alabaster eggs, shells, polished stones and china shepherdesses, because the small space was filled by two hard leather chairs and a hard leather settee, all draped with crocheted antimacassars, arm protectors and cushions. On the mantelpiece was a clunking clock, and a very old wedding photograph, in which Mrs Morgan (presumably), stood in 1920s glory.

On the walls hung Victorian prints of impossibly sweet children and small animals. In one corner stood a small old TV on a dark wooden table and in the other a standard lamp with a green shade glared out even though the ceiling light was also on. The curtains were cream with huge roses all over them, the carpet was pinkly floral and a semi-circular hearthrug clashed in orange and brown. The fire itself was blazing with heat. After being outside for an hour, it felt as if we'd walked into a furnace. There really was no need to tell us to keep away. Although... on the beige hearth tiles was something that looked a little like a cradle. Only, it was made of metal and rattled.

We sat squashed up on the settee, waiting for Mrs Morgan, and rummaged through our hoard. It was disappointing. The reward for all our efforts was 50p in coppers, a handful of boiled sweets, some of which appeared to have been in the back of a drawer for a very very long time, and a packet of those black cough lozenges that, tasting simultaneously of pepper, liquorice, tar and medicine can take the back off your throat after two sucks. So much for a pound each to spend at Woolworths.

As much as it was possible to loll back in disappointment, we did. Suddenly the metal cradle shook so hard it twisted on the hearth and smoke burst out.

'Mrs Morgan! Mrs Morgan! Your baby's on fire!' shouted my little sister before logic could kick in or I could kick her.

Mrs Morgan came bustling in with a tray and put it down on a side table then turning to stand between us and the fire. Bending over, she muttered into the cradle. The smoke and rattling lessened and she straightened up, turning to face us with her hands on her hips.

'Don't worry, lovely,' she said to my sister, 'it's not a baby. Have some cocoa. Anyway, what you got then?'

She peered into our hoard and tutted. 'That's a shame, that is. Who gave you them barley twists? Look ancient, they do. Them lozenges mind, do you want them?'

We all shook our heads.

'Can I have them then?'

We nodded.

'Have you got a sore throat, Mrs Morgan?' asked Ffion's sister.

'No, lovely, but they're spicy and I'm after spicy things at the moment.'

I delved into my satchel, 'Do you want this then?' I asked, pulling out the bottle Dad had given me. Its contents swirled in dull brown opacity and sediment rose in murky clumps as I handed it over.

Mrs Morgan took it with some trepidation.

'What is it?'

'Dad's home-made ginger-beer. He thought we ought to have something warming to drink as we went round.'

'That's weird that is,' said Mrs Morgan, shaking the bottle, 'walking round with drinks. Who'd want to do that?'

As she unscrewed the top, the room filled with the scent of ginger and yeast. The cradle started rattling again and more smoke than ever billowed out.

'Hush now,' Mrs Morgan murmured. Then she said 'what's it taste like?'

I struggled for words. Truth to tell, it tasted better than it looked, but only just. And only if you like ginger. 'Hot.' I concluded.

'You're the girl from that house with all them books aren't you?' she said to me. 'Seen them all piled up in your front room. Are there any about dragons?'

'Well, I'm not sure about Dad, but *I've* got some about dragons.'

'Welsh dragons?'

'Cornish.'

'Cornish dragons indeed.' Mrs Morgan hesitated and looked over her shoulder at the hearth. 'Can I trust you lot?' She seemed to be asking herself as much as she was asking us.

We all nodded and tried to sit up straight.

'Come and look then.'

With some difficulty we extracted ourselves from the settee. Ffion and I levering ourselves up by leaning on our little sisters so that we got out first.

Inside the metal cradle was a small dragon, not quite a foot in length. It was squirming around and lashing its tail. Glaring up at us with red eyes, it opened its jaws and huffed out a mouthful of smoke which stung our eyes.

Mrs Morgan reached inside and lifted it out, holding it like a cat. It rested its head against her chest and scowled.

'Touch him,' she said, 'he's not long hatched. I found the egg in the woods. Thought it was a pretty stone and was going to get my grandson to polish it up for me.'

He was soft, like the leather on a ballet shoe, and while he felt hot to start with, I could feel him cooling.

'I need something to feed him. Nothing I've got seems to do the trick. I thought I could try some of those lozenges.'

Sitting down, she put the dragon in her lap and opened the packet, taking one out and feeding it with finger and thumb be-tween the needle-sharp teeth. We all tensed as he went very still. I held my sister's hand. After all, if anything happened to her, it would somehow be my fault. Every now and then a forked tongue flicked out as the dragon rolled his eyes. The thrashing of his tail stopped and we saw him swallow. There was a pause, before he looked up at Mrs Morgan and opened his mouth. She popped an-other lozenge in. The dragon actually sighed. Pink smoke came out of his snout and he relaxed.

'Can you put a bit of ginger beer in a saucer for me lovely?' she said to Ffion.

Ffion poured out a little and held it towards the dragon. He drank it before we could blink. Blue smoke swirled with the pink and spiralled up to the ceiling.

'Feel him now!' said Mrs Morgan.

He was like a hot water bottle. His eyes were closing and he curled up with his tail over his nose.

'What are you going to do with him, Mrs Morgan?' asked Ffion.

'No idea. But I'll need to work out how to get him back in case his mother comes looking. Only I need to leave him safe. Can you imagine what them boys could do if they found him?'

I was busy imagining what a dragon could do to the boys.

'You girls have been wonderful. No telling mind.'

We shook our heads.

Mrs Morgan popped the sleeping dragon back into the cradle, left the room and came back with her purse.

'Here's 20p each,' she said.

'You can't give us that!' I exclaimed.

'Take is as payment for the ginger-beer,' she answered, 'now off home with you, it's getting late.'

Back home I asked Dad if he had any books on dragons. The good thing about Dad was that nothing was ever an odd question if it involved reading. We surveyed the front room with its bulging bookcases and stacks of un-shelved volumes. I could see the glint in his eyes and decided I'd leave him to undertake the quest on his own.

'Did you bring back ginger-beer bottle?' he asked as he starting poking about.

'Oh she liked it so much, Mrs Morgan bought it from us,' I said. 'I think she preferred it to our singing.'

'Do you think she'd like the recipe?'

'I'm sure of it,' I answered, 'I'll take it round tomorrow with a Christmas card.'

'It's been a strange sort of evening,' he said, muffled behind a large tome, 'only Mrs Price was round earlier to check you lot were all right. She said her lads went up into the woods after they'd been carol-singing and came running back saying there was something stamping around and the trees were smouldering. I assumed they were covering up because they'd been setting fires again. Did you see anything unusual while you were out?'

'N-no. But Dad?'

'Yes?'

'Have we still got that chilli powder you said was too hot? Only I might just pop out with it just now. I have a feeling Mrs Morgan might need it before tomorrow.'

Christmas Pudding

Miss Jemima Maplin was just about to sip the cocoa brought by her trusted maid, Bea, when her reverie was disturbed by the ringing of the telephone bell.

'Ma'am!' exclaimed Bea, 'it's a call from Lady Simpleton-Smythe. She says please to come at once! There's been a murder at the Hall.'

Really, thought Miss Maplin, the lower orders get themselves so excited over small matters.

'Do calm down, Bea. Tell Lady Simpleton-Smythe I will be with her directly, then order me a taxi. I will collect my knitting and put on my sensible coat. Oh and put a hot water bottle in my bed when I am gone, I may be a little late home.'

As she sat in the back of the taxi going up the long drive to Simpleton Hall, Miss Maplin considered the play of the moonlight on the bushes within the gates. At the door, Miss Maplin noted that she was not greeted, as was the norm, by Sidle the butler, but that the door had been opened by the head housemaid. However, being well-bred, she expressed no surprise and having been divested of her coat asked to be taken to see her friend.

Lady Lavinia Simpleton-Smythe was in the drawing room, standing by the fire and wringing her hands. Miss Maplin's eyes quickly swept the room. The room had been tastefully decorated for the festive season and candles sparkled from the chandelier onto the four gilt cherubs standing in various poses on the mantlepiece. In various chairs and sofas, the weekend guests sat looking somewhat put out, smoking or sipping cocktails. Miss Maplin spotted Lady Simpleton-Smythe's son from her earlier marriage: the Hon Bertie Littlebrain. Nearby were Bertie's film star fiancee Fi-fi Cherche-D'or and a dubious looking person called Ivor Loanforu whom she remembered was 'In Trade', reputed to be foreign and therefore not a gentleman. Someone was missing.

'Jemima!' cried Lavinia, rushing to clasp her friend's hands, 'thank goodness you've come. You'll never guess what has happened!'

'I imagine that Humphrey has been murdered.'

'How astonishing you are Jemima,' Lavinia gasped, 'however did you guess?'

'My dear, as you telephoned to say someone had been murdered and as Humphrey is clearly not here, I put two and two together. Had it been a servant, I imagine you would have simply called the police.'

'The police are here of course,' Lavinia conceded, 'but really they are so stupid. They seem to want to question all of us. In fact I am not so certain it is murder in any case. And just when I needed to rely on him, Sidle is not here. He received a telegram earlier today apparently, and left without asking permission. Cook says he was somewhat distressed, but really, why his personal concerns should interfere with the running of this house, I cannot imagine. It has left me with only 20 servants and no-one in charge - how is one to manage? Cook has been difficult all day. Never mind, do come and see Humphrey and see if you can help the police like you usually do.'

Lord Simpleton-Smythe was spreadeagled on his front in the dining room. He had not yet dressed for dinner and was still in his tweeds, his usually red bombastic face was drained. His blood, along with what appeared to be a very small amount of brain, had in fact drained into the rug and was rather spoiling the pattern.

'That carpet has been in this family for generations,' Lavinia sighed, looking down on her husband's lifeless form, 'I don't suppose the maids will be able to get the stain out unless we can move him quickly and the police won't let us. Even then, it's the sort of thing maids give notice for. They just don't like the hard work these days. But do look - there's a pistol in his hand, he must have done it himself, although I can't imagine why.'

Miss Maplin looked carefully round the room. This too was decorated for Christmas and the table was laid for dinner. A candelabrum in the centre of the table lit up the silver and crystal-ware pleasantly. She noted that the shield on the wall was somewhat awry, as was the hunting scene on the adjacent wall.

'Lavinia,' she asked, 'why is there a Christmas pudding on the floor by the sideboard?'

Lavinia turned from her contemplation of the chalk marks around her husband's body, which were reasonably certain to be removable, and looked in surprise at the Christmas pudding which was lying up against a small dent in the skirting board.

'My goodness,' she said, ringing for a maid and summoning cook.

Cook arrived at the same time as Inspector Meticulose. Cook looked somewhat defiant when the pudding was pointed out to her.

'It's like this, my lady,' she said, 'the master told Sidle that he was not satisfied with last year's Christmas pudding and insisted on Sidle bringing this year's up for inspection. He said… he said… if it was as inedible as before, I might be dismissed.' Cook started to sob.

Miss Maplin patted the Cook gently and asked softly, 'I see that the pudding is not quite round. Are you experimenting with the new shape?'

Cook stopped crying and drew herself up, 'certainly not, ma'am. A pudding isn't a pudding unless it's round… but come to think of it, that does look a bit flat on a couple of sides. Fancy - it wasn't like that when I gave it to Sidle.'

'I don't suppose it had silver thread on it either.'

'No indeed.'

'Very well, you may go,' said Miss Maplin, 'now, Lavinia, do go and sit down with your guests and have a stiff brandy. I'm sure you must be quite distrait. I just want a few words with the Inspector.'

Lavinia withdrew somewhat reluctantly and the Inspector drew up a chair for his old ally Miss Maplin.

'Out with it, Ma'am,' said the Inspector, 'I assume you realise it wasn't suicide. To start with, he's holding the pistol in the wrong hand and secondly, there is no residue. Presumably you also have some knowledge of how Lord Simpleton-Smythe's death will benefit everyone.'

'Well,' said Miss Maplin, settling back with her knitting, careful to ensure the wool didn't fall into the pool of blood, 'Humphrey was a dreadful bully and held the purse strings tight. It meant that Bertie couldn't finance his fiancée's play and without finance, it's doubtful anyone would put her on the stage where she would actually have to act. Meanwhile, I imagine she is withholding her favours until she's sure of Bertie's securing a fortune worth marrying him for. However, there may be another reason why money is not forthcoming. In fact, I suspect Mr Loanforu is here either to reclaim monies owed or to advance more.'

Inspector Meticulose nodded with respect.

'Quite right on all sides, Miss Maplin. Add into that mixture the fact that his Lordship was embezzling the servants' Christmas fund and it seems that Sidle discovered this when he asked for an advance. Sidle told the footman that he was going to approach his Lordship because he was in some trouble. He didn't say what. I have to say that the staff don't seem too worried that he's disappeared, in fact they seem very pleased, especially the younger maids.'

Miss Maplin nodded to herself.

'Inspector,' she said, 'I suggest that you get your men to search the bushes just inside the gate. I am quite certain that you will find Sidle there. I am afraid he is most likely to be dead. In his possession, you will find three gold cherubs from the set currently on the mantlepiece in the drawing room. I remember there were seven of them, last Christmas. There have been rumours about his tendencies for a number of years. I imagine that he wanted an advance to buy off a young woman whom he'd got into trouble.'

The Inspector was astonished: 'Do you mean….. the butler did it? And how do you know he's dead in the bushes? What could have happened here?'

'Look around you, Inspector,' said Miss Maplin, frowning over a complicated slip one, purl one, 'Humphrey was weighing up the Christmas pudding in his hand when Sidle shot him. As he fell, with great presence of what was left of his mind, Humphrey threw the Christmas pudding at Sidle. It struck Sidle hard (Cook does make rather heavy puddings), causing him a fatal head injury and then bounced off him onto the shield and from the shield to the painting on the adjacent wall, finally coming to rest, still bearing one of Sidle's grey hairs, and given its velocity and mass, denting the skirting board. Sidle had sufficient time to snatch the cherubs while the guests were changing for dinner and make his escape, but the injury sustained overtook him before he left the grounds. I could just make him out as I passed in the taxi.'

The Inspector whistled softly.

'You really are amazing Miss Maplin. You should be in the force. Well, neither man is a great loss I suppose.'

'No indeed,' Miss Maplin agreed, 'and in the end…. both of them got their just desserts.'

Donkey

I'm glad you came to me. Come and have a look. Yes, I know he looks a bit weatherbeaten but he's a good donkey. He won't let you down.

Let me tell you about him while you look him over. I was very young when I first knew him. My father was a vicious man and used to beat him; used to beat me too, but not as badly. This poor donkey, he was only young but there's only so much abuse any of us can take, isn't there? One day, it was just too much and he collapsed in the road. My father whipped him and kicked him. I remember crying out for him to stop, but - see those scars on his nose and shoulder - that was from that day. This poor donkey just lay there, too weak with hunger to do anything except bray. I thought he would die in the dust. There was a priest about and he remonstrated with my father, it is written that you should treat your livestock well. Well even in a rage, my father wasn't stupid enough to contradict a priest, but he aimed one final kick at the donkey and said it was a useless animal and asked if anyone would buy it. Well no-one was going to buy this poor bleeding pathetic beast but then a stranger came up and said that he would. A real stranger. Not someone from another town - an outsider, an immigrant, you know, one of *those* people. The priest said father wasn't to trade with him, that his money would be unclean and father looked down at the half dead beast and said the stranger could have him for nothing. The donkey was worthless anyway. As he walked home, hauling me out of my hiding place, he said aside to the bystanders 'they probably eat them you know.' He took his temper out on me later and then started on my mother, but it was the last thing he did - dropped down dead when he went to strike her again. The priests said it was a judgment for trading with that outsider, even though no money changed hands. They never said it was a judgment for being a violent monster.

Mother and I were fortunate. We were taken into my uncle's household and since my aunt had no sons, in the end I was taught the family business and we were happy. One day, I had to travel to another town to talk business.

It was a dangerous route, but I was young and confident, taking care to travel in broad daylight and keep my wits about me. But there was only me. And young as I was, I was no match for the bandits in those mountains. They ambushed me, they kicked and punched me and took everything I had, leaving me for dead. I thought it was the end, but I didn't die. After a while, two people passed by, one after another; people from town who constantly told everyone how we should live and what we should do. I couldn't move, but each saw me and came close - not close enough to check if I was alive - and I was unable to speak so I couldn't call to them. I could just make them out through my swollen eyelids as they scampered away, frightened to get too close in case they came into contact with death. I thought what a terrible way to die it was, crushed and broken and bleeding with no-one to care.

People say you relive your past in your final moments and I thought it was happening to me, because blurry as my vision was, I could see the muzzle of that donkey from my childhood, a little greyer perhaps, but I recognised the scar on his nose and could just make out one on his shoulder.

Then I heard a voice, a stranger's voice. The words were spoken in a foreign accent, but the stranger was comforting me, telling me he would take care of me and he lifted me up from the dirt, bloody and filthy as I was, and he took me home on the back of this donkey and cared for me until I was better. Before I went home, I begged to buy the donkey from him. It seemed like we belonged together. And when I look at him I remember this: you can say all the right things, but if you don't live up to it, then the words are worthless.

Yosef, I've known you since you were a lad. I know what they're saying about you. But the people who say those things are full of their own self-righteousness, whereas you're a decent man, kind and devout, and everyone can see you love your wife, despite what they're saying about her too.

So, I'm on your side: because being a decent person isn't down to who you are, or where you're from, or what you say, but how you actually behave. Take the donkey, Yosef, treat him well. He's still strong enough to carry Miryam; she can't walk all that way in her condition. And when your child is old enough, you tell him the donkey's story and what it means. Maybe one day, he'll pass it on too.

Toy Soldier

As the night fell on Christmas Eve, Alf, leaning against the wall, closed his eyes and thought of home. Alf's family were chapel, and didn't hold with fuss. But they would be settling down for the evening, filling the little ones' stockings. Bert's family next door would be getting ready to go to the midnight service at the church, yawning, unaccustomed to staying up late. Bert's sister would be beautiful in the lamplight.

Alf looked over to their captain, a young gentleman from the big house in their village. Alf and Bert had been brought up to respect their betters but looking at the terrified, twitching wreck, Alf realised that he was just a man; they were all just men, trying to do their best in the middle of a nightmare they had not imagined and could not escape.

That Christmas Eve, Alf and Bert looked over the edge of their trench at the candles edging the German lines. Their ears ached from listening for bullets which didn't come. All that could be heard were carols and the occasional greeting. Alf closed his eyes, pretending that he would wake soon and find himself in his bedroom with his brothers.

On Christmas morning, the soldiers from both sides mingled, trying to feel festive. Alf, Bert and the other young men played football with lads from the German army. Somewhere deep inside the thought bubbled up: whatever it was they were fighting about - couldn't they just settle it with a game of football and go home? Alf slipped in the mud and crashed down with the young German he was tackling. The ball skidded off over the lumpy soil and for a brief moment, he and his enemy caught eyes, laughing as they tried to help each other up, their boots silted and heavy.

On Christmas afternoon, the orders came to start fighting again.

Alf saw one of the Germans catch a bullet and fall. His friend going to help him, briefly looked up and caught Alf's eye.

Alf lowered his gun. It was the lad from the football match. In those seconds of recognition, someone else's bullet did what Alf couldn't do.

When Bert fell, Alf didn't hesitate.

Perhaps, right now, Bert's sister was looking at Alf's Christmas gift and smiling. She wouldn't smile if she knew that Alf was hauling Bert's body into a trench in the middle of a muddy field with smashed tree trunks like tomb stones. Maybe she'd never smile again. Or maybe she would fall into his arms and her tears would heal him.

Some soldiers called Alf brave because he showed no fear, crawling under fire to bring Bert back. Soldiers from his own pals' battalion just thought he was trying to make up for his brother Fred who refused to enlist. Fred said killing was wrong - there had to be better ways to resolve things. People said Fred was a coward.

Alf knew Fred was the bravest and wisest of all of them.

Three Wise Men

There are a few things most people don't realise about the three wise men. For a start, they ended up wiser than they started, that is, when they stopped equating value with wealth. Secondly there were four of them and of those four, two were woman, so you had: Caspar, Melchior, Belle and Shazza. Thirdly, after they returned home, they studied for a lot longer and became time travellers and fourthly...

Sorry - did you hear right? Time travellers? Yes that's right. Your ancient world research scientist had a lot more time on their hands, more money if they kept on the right side of the right people and didn't have to worry about quite so many rules and regulations. OK, so there tended to be a bit more collateral damage (eyebrows, buildings, servants) but they thought it was a price worth paying.

After a few experiments like revisiting last Tuesday to work out where Melchior had put that scroll on alchemy or getting Belle to rethink the purchase of that robe in cerise with lime green mystical squiggles; they decided to work out if there was some practical purpose for their skill.

So they looked back and forth in history to see if at any point mankind had ever valued kindness and love and forgiveness over power and wealth and celebrity and discovered that in every generation, as a whole, they didn't. Those who did made a massive impact but received little recognition. It was quite a depressing exercise and although their quest continued, after a while they decided to take a break and be time-tourists instead.

Now it has to be said that the wise men (and women) were fairly self-absorbed and the day that they travelled into the 21st Century and discovered internet search engines was a happy one. Once they found out that they were remembered in scripture and legend, they spent a glorious day or so, looking themselves up and noting down everything that the internet had wrong.

Then they discovered Nativity Plays.

For a whole month, they gorged on Nativity Plays. Primary schools, churches, pre-schools, nurseries, you name it, they were there. How did they get in? Well using a bit of additional time travel to check audience criteria and edit guest lists and a really good desk top publishing package to make tickets, they managed to squeeze themselves in as random relatives and sat at the back, munching on sweets and nudging each other when the Three Wise Men came on.

They liked it best when they were Three *Kings* of course. Then their chests would swell with pride (which was somewhat alarming in Shazza's case) and they would swagger as much as is possible when sitting in a chair designed for a six year old. Of course Belle and Shazza were disappointed that they'd been merged into one person and that person male, but then the one thing they'd noticed in their time travelling was the tendency for this sort of thing throughout history. They were also more than a little baffled by the very modern plays where the three wise men were octopuses or some such. But.... and here we come to the fourth thing people don't realise.

'There they go again,' complained Melchior, picking a bit of popcorn out of his beard, 'Gold for kingliness, check; Myrrh for suffering, check; Incense for holiness, check (though we really do have to find out why they keep bringing in that bloke with the bolts through his neck) but every time they forget the fourth gift!'

Caspar nodded, 'I know, and it was the thing that poor couple appreciated most right at that moment.'

'Took me ages too,' Shazza put in, 'well, ages to get the servants to make it.'

'You're not wrong,' Belle sighed, whispering because the grandmother in front of her had turned to glare, 'I mean, the other three gifts were symbolic and would also be also dead handy in the future. But that's not what you need after a long journey, a disappointing arrival and childbirth. And we knew that, because we were wise. I wish they wouldn't leave the fourth gift out.'

'Aye,' Melchior agreed nostalgically, 'and it was a delicious casserole too.'

Bethlehem

The petrol ran out at the top of the hill. Anne put on the handbrake and looked down onto the tiny hamlet, secret in the falling light, making out its scattered houses and chapel. Polly leaned forward in her car seat tried to read the place name 'B-e-t... what does it say Mummy?' It was the first time she'd spoken all day, sleeping then waking then sleeping.

'It says Bethlehem, sweetie, that's what the village is called.'

'Bethlehem? Really? Is baby Jesus here? And Mary and Joseph and the Angels?'

'It's a different Bethlehem I'm afraid,' said Anne, 'just ordinary people here.'

Polly sat back in disappointment. Bethlehem - Bible story book Bethlehem with its flat roofs, its star, its golden moment of God with us, the hope of a new start; modern Bethlehem with its poverty and graffiti and discord; now this incongruously named green leafy valley, faded under the December dusk. Anne supposed there were Bethlehems all over the world. Still, there was nothing for it now. No way back and only one way forward. She put the car in gear and coasted down the hill.

The road bottomed out at the end of the houses. There was no-one around, all the houses closed up and snug. The car came to a halt next to a gate in a field and a dilapidated sign saying 'caravan for hire'.

'Is there no room at the inn, Mummy?' asked Polly, through her thumb.

'I don't think there's even an inn,' said Anne.

She smoothed Polly's cheek and looked round at the baby who was stirring in his seat. He would need feeding soon. He probably needed changing miles ago.

'Wait here a minute, I just want to check...'

'Me too, me too!' Polly cried, struggling with her harness.

Anne came round and lifted her out and over the gate, then she climbed over and looked at the caravan behind the hedge. It had seen better days. Much better days. But it would do.

'Quietly now,' she whispered to Polly, 'I'm just getting Jack.'

Checking there was still no-one watching, she left Polly anxiously clasping the gate while she climbed over and got the baby and their small collection of sleeping bags and clothes. It was a struggle to get back over the gate with Jack but she did it. Breaking into the caravan took seconds.

'Is this like the stable?' whispered Polly, 'it's smelly.'

The caravan smelled of mustiness and dust, but it wasn't actually damp. Anne gave Polly some more bread and some crisps. There was nothing else. She fed Jack. Polly had been bottle fed but it wasn't an option with Jack and they had had to learn together. Luckily Jack was a good baby, contented and sleepy. Now that she was used to it, the warmth and the rhythm of suckling comforted her as much as it comforted Jack. With her free arm, Anne cuddled Polly.

'It'll be all right,' she whispered.

'Will Daddy come and hit you?' Polly whispered back.

'No,' Anne said firmly, 'we're a long way away and he can't find us now.'

Anne was woken in the morning by Polly's laughter. She hadn't heard it for so long.

'It's a yeg! A yeg!' she was giggling.

Anne raised her head from the bed where she was lying with the children and realised Polly was sitting up and pointing at the end of the bed. There was a chicken wandering around and an egg had been deposited on the sleeping bag. She looked round and saw that the door she had broken open was ajar and another chicken was just poking her head round to see what was happening.

And then the door opened properly. A middle aged woman peered inside and stared at them in surprise.

'There's a yeg!' Polly pointed out.

Anne sat up and lifted Jack up, his downy head heavy with sleep, his baby smell mingling with the smell of unaired caravan and chickens.

'I... I'm sorry,' she said to the strange woman, 'we just needed somewhere to sleep. I can pay for the damage.'

Actually she couldn't. Why had she said that?

The woman blinked a little and then said 'you could have knocked - I'd have put you up inside. This caravan's barely suitable for the chickens. Why didn't you knock?'

Anne paused. All of a sudden, it was too much, the sudden realisation she couldn't take the blows and the insults any more, that she didn't want Polly growing up thinking that was what she deserved, that she didn't want Jack growing up thinking that was how to behave; the guilt - how could she support them? Would they be damaged without a father? The adrenalin of the escape had run out. And the money had run out too. What had she been thinking?

He had been right. She was a terrible mother and a useless woman. She deserved everything she got.

Falteringly she confessed: 'I haven't any money. I couldn't pay for a B&B.'

Tears ran down her face but in her exhaustion she couldn't feel them anymore.

Polly reached up and said 'don't cry Mummy, remember, we're a long way away and Daddy can't find us,' and tried to wipe the tears away.

The strange woman perused at them. She seemed a straightforward sort: short grey hair, comfortable clothes, no make-up. She raised her eyebrows a little but not much. There was a long long pause.

'I'm Susan,' said the strange woman, 'I could do with a hand in the B&B over Christmas. If you like, we could get this caravan habitable for you and the children; if you're willing to help me out? Have a think and come up to the house when you're ready. Whatever you decide I'll have breakfast waiting for you.'

She withdrew and the door closed.

For a while, Anne and the children sat, still huddled on the bed. Then Polly asked softly: 'Is she a Bethlehem angel Mummy? Is she? Is she?'

Drum

Hjalmar cursed the dragon as it struggled against being chained up, angry sparks issuing from its snout. They could never be fully tamed, dragons, no matter how many goblins you fed to them.

Still, he couldn't blame it for being fractious. The battle had been intense, the hordes nearly overwhelming. But even though for a long time it had seemed impossible, finally Hjalmar had achieved his goals and overcome his obstacles. Now, all he needed was some mead to quaff, the proud loving of a good woman and the admiration of his son. Shame that the best he'd get was some mead.

Shouldering his trophies, Hjalmar made his way across the snowy courtyard to the long house. Out of the corner of his eye, he could see a couple of goblins peering round the door of the smaller house which he'd built out of necessity in the corner of the compound. Unearthly sounds were coming from it, delighting the discord-loving goblins. Apart from a heavy incessant hammering, the noise was much as a wolf sounds when it has caught something more sensitive than a foot in a trap combined with the howls of Garmr and the maniacal laughter of a drunken Orc.

Scowling, Hjalmar pushed his way awkwardly into the long house and greeted his wife Magnhild.

'Behold! Your man returns victorious!'

Magnhild looked up from her weaving and raised her eyebrows.

'Took you long enough.'

'It was as if Ragnarök had broken out! I....'

'Serves you right for leaving all your Yuletide shopping until Yuletide Eve,' replied Magnhild, unimpressed, 'I bet there wasn't a decent Yule log to be had. And if you've got me a gift as rubbish as the last two years, you can sleep with the dragon.'

'Woman - mind your tongue. You should be grateful that I still shower you with gifts after all these years, now that your beauty, once legendary .....' Hjalmar watched his wife slowly narrow her eyes and remembered who did the cooking, '....has become enhanced with the years so that you are now as lovely as Freyja!'

He lowered the Yule Log next to the hearth and went to hide his gifts. Unconsciously he rubbed his head. There were still small dents where the year before's hastily bought spindle had struck him after being thrown across the room. It was very strange. If she had bought him an axe, he'd have been thrilled. Why didn't women feel the same about housewife stuff?

From the outbuilding came a particularly loud bit of hammering and Soini could be hear shrieking: 'We are NOT anarchists!' in time with the rhythm.

Hjalmar jumped up from his seat by the fire and burst outside and yelled: 'we ARE anarchists! We're Norse men - feared around the world! What's the point of being a Norse Man if you follow rules!'

The music such as it was continued without pause. Hjalmar went back indoors.

'Put your weaving down, come round my side and have some mead,' he said, 'it might numb your ears.'

They snuggled up by the fire and smirked silently as they thought of the gifts they'd got each other.

Hjalmar thought: 'she's bound to be happy this year. She likes new ideas and new things. That Loki had some tales to tell from his trip to that place he sailed to far off to the South West. Potaytas or something and that chilli stuff he says will warm you right up. Funny name that. Chilli making you hot! I'll pop some in her breakfast!'

He sniggered into his drinking horn.

Magnhild thought: 'When he feels his present he'll think I've got him the finest elf made chain mail. Can't wait to see his face when he opens it to see it's a chain mail mankini. Serves him right for that two piece he got me last year.'

She giggled softly.

As they settled down on the spear side of the fire and started quaffing, a particularly loud bit of hammering and a shrill sound filtered through the thick walls from the other house. The boys sounded as if they were being tortured.

'What happened to the old tunes, that's what I'd like to know?' sighed Hjalmar.

Magnhild sighed too.

Hjalmar continued: 'We used to sing about brave warriors and monsters and occasionally the blood drying on the face of a beautiful warrior maiden (such as yourself) but young people today - what they call music! I don't know. And that incessant hammering - it's worse than being struck repeatedly on the head with a broadsword. How's he managing to make so much noise on his own?'

'Bjorn and Kjeld are over. Bjorn's got a lyre and Kjeld has a flute of some kind. They're a band. They're trying to think up a name.'

'I could think of a few.' Hjalmar grunted, 'Shouldn't they be practising their fighting?'

'They say that fighting is a product of a defunct older generation afraid of confronting its own demons.'

'What does that mean exactly?'

'No idea,' Magnhild answered, peering closely at her mead, 'but I got Soini a drum for Yule. It's got to be better than listening to him hitting that anvil all the time.'

Hjalmar grimmaced. It was hard to imagine it being any worse, but you never knew.

Bauble

When I left that December morning, it was so early that there wasn't even a hint of the dawn. The town was in pitch darkness and the road of of town even darker.

I felt as if I were still asleep, in the middle of one of my stress dreams. Trees and hedges loomed blacker than the blackness. I waited for the dream to develop like it usually does - the accelerator pedal stuck, the car lights faltering then failing, the brakes not responding. But I was not dreaming, it was simply too early and too misty for there to be any light.

On the high ground, the mist turned into fog, thick and clinging. The car, a lonely bubble on the coast road slicing through ancient slopes and hill forts, could have been the only car. I felt like the only person awake in the whole world.

Around 6.45, I had to stop. I was struggling to stay awake and still had a long way to go. I didn't know quite where I was, but yellow, red and white lights suddenly appeared out of the fog on the hilltop ahead. I thought maybe someone had left their outside decorations on, it was nearly Christmas after all. But I was wrong. Of all the things to find along a road of traditional English pubs, here was an American style diner, its 'open' sign flashing in pink neon.

I pulled up, longing for coffee and a bacon roll, hoping, since I'm not a morning person, that the customer service would not be as cheerful as the decor. That's fine at lunchtime, but first thing, all you want is someone as monosyllabic as you feel.

A solemn looking woman greeted me as I passed the Christmas tree inside the entrance, admiring its subtle decorations and twinkling lights. They seemed out of keeping with the primary vibrancy of the rest of the room.

The woman directed me to a table and left me to peruse the menu. I was glad of the silence, finding the previous day's morning papers to read. After a while, a younger woman came up to take my order.

'We've got specials' she told me.

It seemed rude not to ask what they were.

'Honey cakes and mulled beer,' the waitress said. I blinked and looked to see if she was joking, but she didn't seem to be.

'Honey cakes sound nice,' I admitted, 'but I'm not sure drinking beer first thing in the morning is a good idea.'

'It's not strong. The herbs will invigorate you,' she coaxed, 'it's more like a sort of spiced porridge than a drink.'

Couldn't say that exactly sold it. While I was trying to think of a polite response, the older woman came up. She held one of the baubles from the Christmas tree. It was a sort of dull silver and blue. Light caught on intricate golden markings. It was the loveliest thing, far too nice for its surroundings.

'I could see you liked it,' said the waitress, 'it's for sale. I wonder if you'd like a closer look.'

For a moment, I was tempted. I could feel my hand raising to touch it. The stronger the urge became, the more the smell of toast receded and was replaced by the scent of herbs, honey, wood smoke and the gaudy colours of the diner faded as the room started to darken and it seemed as if on the one side of me was the heat of a fire and on the other a draught subtly carrying the smell of the sea. The bauble sparkled and in its curve I could see the two waitresses reflected but their images were not in red and yellow nylon uniforms but in cloaks of brown and green, their faces eager.

Then some vehicle or other crashed its gears outside and broke my concentration. I didn't need any more decorations and this one looked expensive. Honey cakes sounded nice, but I prefer savoury for breakfast and no way was I having beer. Don't like it at the best of times.

'It's OK thanks,' I said, 'I'll just have coffee and a bacon roll.'

The room came back into focus and the waitresses exchanged glances and went away.

I waited quite a while and there was no sign of activity, so after a bit, I went up to the counter and called out. No one came, so, somewhat annoyed, I gave up and left. I still had two hours of driving and I'd get coffee at the next garage instead.

On the way back, it was still foggy but not yet dark, so I decided to stop at the diner, maybe try the honey cakes and ask what had happened to my breakfast.

The man behind the counter looked baffled, 'only special we had today was a turkey curry at lunchtime. Never even heard of honey cakes. Don't remember seeing you either, and I've been here all day. When did you come in?'

'About quarter to seven I guess,' I told him, 'two waitresses took my order.'

'Think you've got the wrong place, love,' he responded, 'we don't open till half seven. And there's only me and Dave working here.'

I looked around. It was the only American style diner on this road. The Christmas tree looked different. There were just the usual multi-coloured lights and wonky fairy.

'I thought there were baubles on your tree,' I said.

'Nah - kids used to keep nicking them, so we haven't bothered for years. Tell you what, it's this fog, creeps you out don't it? Some of the old folks say things come to get you in this fog and you're never seen again. Don't know what sort of things. Are you all right, love? Here come and sit down for a bit, have a cuppa on the house. Or would you prefer a beer?'

'No,' I said, 'I definitely wouldn't prefer a beer.'

Angels

See the Angels. Neither male nor female, unbothered by distractions of hunger, or desire or ageing, the Angels watch.

See the Angels: they are here to show you what is real and what is important.

Look: they are standing by that man in the doorway. The one in the sleeping bag, lying on cardboard, who hasn't even the energy to beg from you. The Angels are pointing at him, but your eyes are sliding by. You see a wreck, a waste of space, someone who's thrown his life away, a scrounger. And it's not so cold this winter, he'll be fine. The Angels see what the man was, what he could be, what brought him to lie gaunt and dirty without even the energy to beg.

See the Angels: they are standing on the bridge next to that girl who's leaning over. She is swaying slightly. She has lost one of her shoes and the other is in her hand. The Angels are pointing at her but your eyes are sliding by. You see a girl who's drunk or drugged too much at a party. If you get too close, she might cry or vomit, if she's not careful she's going to fall into that river. The Angels see a girl who feels lost, for whom the future is like the mouth of a monster yet the swirling depths as welcoming as a cosy bed in which she can sleep dreamlessly.

Look: the Angels are by the old lady on the bus stop. She doesn't have much in her shopping bag. Her tights have bunched at her ankles and her coat looks drab. The Angels point at her and she smiles at you but your eyes are sliding by. You see a mad old bat who will probably jibber at you and dribble maybe. She might follow you home if you talk to her. The Angels see a lonely woman, bright as a button, funny as they come, just wanting to chat for a few moments to remind herself she still exists.

See the Angels: they are standing by that man with tears in his eyes. The Angels point at him, but your eyes are sliding by. That man is usually the life and soul; it will bring you down if you speak to him. He's got plenty going for him, nothing to complain about. The Angels see someone who knows he is losing someone, who just wants a friend to see him through.

Your eyes keep sliding by as you rush to spend your money on more presents and more food but you won't see the Angels in the shops. They will be at the hospital, in the graveyard, at the soup kitchen, in the prison cell and refugee camp.

The Angels are here to show you want is real and what is important. To show you how to be the hand and heart of God. But you cannot see them.

Can you?

Candy Cane

Kieran was not a fan of Christmas, or at least, not a fan of the self-indulgent excess, consumerism and sentiment which seemed to be at its core. Light in the darkness he could handle.

The office Christmas party filled him with dread. For a start, he took great care of his body and ate organic vegan food and consumed minimal alcohol. Secondly, parties weren't his thing anyway. He preferred a pleasant evening with people capable of holding a conversation and appreciating a nice meal. Still, Kieran didn't want his colleagues to think he was totally anti-social or lacking in Christmas spirit. With some embarrassment, he agreed to wear a Christmas outfit, settling for a jumper with 'Bah Humburger' on it. Get it? - an anti-Christmas vegan with a hamburger?... no never mind. Nita did though, he saw her grin when he came in. She was dressed as a candy cane. Or at least that was what she'd aimed for. She was certainly stripy. Only short and busty rather than long and skinny. Nita looked cute, the stripes spiralling round her curves, her hair tied up in a big bow. She was carrying a matching super sized cane to match as well, just in case no-one understood. He got her joke too. Nita was diabetic, last thing she could enjoy was a candy cane. It was the hope that somehow he could work out the right words to start a proper conversation with her that made him stay.

After a couple of hours though, he gave up. Nita had been cornered by Steve the Smarm from marketing and he whatever he was saying to her seemed to be having the right effect.

Kieran slipped out of the office and into the damp, disappointing night.

His route home took him through the Christmas market with its lights and tempting smell of food but he weaved in and out of the customers and headed on. He noticed a couple of hastily set up stalls selling cheaper stuff; stalls that would easily come down if anyone came to check your licence. He passed one selling deep fried turkey burgers with extra lettuce. The extra lettuce intrigued him. The kinds of people who bought food as desperate as those burgers didn't usually worry about their five a day. Although the smell was making him gag, he did peer a little closer and thought how vibrant the lettuce looked, giving the burgers a green glow. The vendor came forward hopefully if a little unsteadily.

'Full up,' lied Kieran, entering the shortcut.

It was a dark and dismal alley. As long as you kept to the middle, you were reasonably sure of not standing in anything or anyone unpleasant. Dark shadows seemed darker than usual, he thought and there was a lot of barely audible groaning going on. Hard to say if it was drunken passion or drunken vomiting. Best to keep straight on.

Halfway down the alley, something attacked him, hauling at this jumper, slashing and biting at his neck. Kieran, taken by surprise, started to overbalance, but managed to right himself, flinging out and somehow making enough contact with the thing's head to shove it away. He could just hear some clattering behind him and had braced himself for an assault from two sides, when he heard Nita shout 'watch out - it's coming for you again!'

He struck out with his fists at the assailant and was aware of Nita flailing around with something. There was a sudden sickening sucking sound and then a thunk and the attacker's body slumped to the floor.

'I don't believe it,' said Nita, her voice trembling, 'I knocked its head clean off! How is that even possible?'

'Quick! Run!' shouted Kieran, grabbing her arm and dragging her down the remainder of the alleyway. He was aware of another shadow moving and coming towards them.

This wasn't the way he'd dreamt it. He'd always hoped that one day Nita would come round to his flat and they'd converse and fall in love. He hadn't expected her to be supporting him as he staggered up the stairs, his one hand pressing on the bite on his neck. He hadn't expected her to be wearing a pretty white and pink striped dress spattered in blood and dragging a chipped and bloody candy cane behind her.

'Good party?' asked his neighbour who passed them on the landing, 'Bit of red wine spillage there. Best get some white on straightaway - it always helps.'

'We need to get you to a hospital,' said Nita, when they got inside and she checked his wound. The jumper had taken the majority of the assault, but there were definite teeth marks and the skin had been broken. The area was bruised and going green.

'And I ought to report to the police...' her eyes filled with tears, 'I don't even like killing beetles and I don't even know what that thing was.'

'Don't worry, it'll be fine. I'll go in the morning. I can't face it now.'

Kieran felt tired. This wasn't how he had wanted it to be, 'why did you come after me?'

'I kept hoping you'd come and rescue me from Steve. Then I saw you go and I thought... I realised... I just wanted to say...' she faltered, 'so I came out to say Happy Christmas and ask if you'd like to, er, there's this concert on Friday, anyway... so I came out and I saw you go past that disgusting burger stall and I was about to give up when I saw something follow you. And then I... Oh I still feel sick. Do you think I'll be arrested? Kieran? Are you all right? Kieran?'

Her voice was fading. The room was disappearing.

The following morning, Kieran got up. Or at least what was left of Kieran. He briefly saw a girl asleep in the armchair but something held him back from touching her. He stumbled out of his front door and down the stairs onto the street. It was heaving. The pavements were thick with shoppers, weaving in and out, getting in each other's way, on each others' feet and tempers. Kieran lurched, his feet dragged, his head lolled. Left to his own devices, he would have moved slowly, but he was swept along in the crowd, his feet barely touching the ground. He tried to make a few lunges at people, but it was impossible. They were moving too fast and they were wearing too many layers. Eventually Kieran managed to traverse the throng and try to re-enter the alleyway which led to the centre of town. There was blue and white tape across it and it took him three attempts to climb over.

Half way down, he noticed a target. It was bent over, looking at something on the ground. Kieran's mind fought for control. Part of him was aware of a throbbing in his neck, of antibodies struggling with a virus, desperate for help. He could see a severed head staring up from the ground and three or four dead bodies scattered around. Another part of him saw a chance to pass the virus on; a living man looking at a headless body, a man whose neck was exposed.

Kieran groaned.

'I know mate,' said the man, without turning round, 'enough to turn your stomach. We think we've got them all though. This one was the only one who might have done any damage we reckon and someone sorted it out good and proper. Just hope it didn't get anyone first. On the other hand, shame we didn't capture it alive so we could get some anti-bodies...'

He turned round and saw, not a colleague, but a dribbling, shuffling, white eyed monster bending over him. His eyes widened in panic and then in surprise, focussing over Kieran's shoulder.

The part of Kieran which was still alive turned and saw a giant candy cane descending with as much force as a five foot woman in a pink and white dress can summon.

....

'We traced the outbreak' were the first words he heard when he came round, 'thank God you didn't manage to kill him and thank God he was still fighting it off - it means we've got the blood we need to stop it spreading.'

Kieran half opened his eyes. He was in a sterile looking room surrounded by people in bio-hazard suits. One of them, shorter than average, the sleeves and legs of her suit bunched up, was presumably Nita. He hoped it was, because she was holding his hand. Admittedly she was wearing a heavy duty glove, but the thought was there.

'What caused it?' Nita asked, stroking his arm gently.

'Some fool had some infected turkeys. Still trying to work out how they got to be radio-active or whatever it is. He thought he'd destroyed them all but one of his employees was a bigger fool and turned a few into burgers. He had a bit of difficulty covering up the fact that they glowed in the dark, but it's amazing what people will eat when they're drunk enough. Fortunately for mankind, if not for them, the majority of people who ate the burgers just died of food poisoning because the burgers hadn't been cooked properly. We've interrogated the vendor and worked out only two people must have become zombies. You killed the one that bit your young man and the other one managed to stagger home.'

'I still feel terrible about killing that first one, it just sort of happened.'

'Don't worry - you did the right thing in the circumstances.'

Nita's gloved hand gently smoothed Kieran's face. He smiled at her.

'So how did you contain it?' she asked.

The scientist explained: 'the other victim and Kieran both set out this morning geared up to spread the infection. If you're going to do that kind of thing you need a bit of space to work in - the other poor chap got swept along by the crowd and lost what was left of his balance by the side of the pavement just as the Christmas parade was going by. Turns out Santa's sleigh is surprisingly good at crushing 100% of the zombies it runs over. It left something of a mess but the elves found some fake snow pretty pronto and got it covered up before anyone noticed. As far as we can work out, that zombie only bit one person, who checked into A&E and we were looking out for it by then and could isolate him. Of course, meanwhile, your Kieran was fighting the infection - perhaps it went against the grain for a vegan - anyway now we've got his blood, we're pretty hopeful we can sort them both out in time for New Year.'

While Kieran opened his eyes to look up at Nita, the scientist leaned over and concluded:

'Thing is, you picked the wrong weekend for a zombie invasion. No-one stands a chance moving slowly on the last Saturday before Christmas. Oh and a word to the wise: don't let your girlfriend take up hockey any time soon - she's lethal.'

Bell

Sometimes they say it's too cold for snow, sometimes that it's too wet. Sometimes the weather just does what it feels like doing.

'Not now, not midwinter,' argued Dan.

Beth ignored him. Another unbearable Christmas would overwhelm her.

'You've still got me, Mum,' Dan said.

But Dan could go to his girlfriend's parents' house. Dan could start making his own traditions. Beth could not resurrect hers without John.

'It's something to do,' she argued, 'I'll raise lots of money for research, so someone else doesn't have to go through what Dad did…what we did.'

'I get that, Mum, but it's madness hiking round the country in December. Do it in Spring and we'll come too.'

But she left anyway, taking her path along the coast John had loved, hoping the bitter salt spray would scour the numbness into life.

When the coast road disappeared or was closed off, she meandered into small towns and country estates, past abandoned farmhouses and old ruins. John had loved it, though she never understood why. He said it summed up why he loved her, his English rose, reserved and indirect, but that didn't help. This dreary old south English countryside was damp and cold. Now its chill possessed her. He had died and her emotions had switched off. She felt nothing. She felt as dull as her surroundings.

Colours were dun, brown, stark. The hedgerows, so deep into winter were barren, frozen into a shadow of their summer memory, their berries all but stripped. The animals were sombre: undertaker crows marched across stubble fields, assassin magpies appeared one at a time - one for sorrow, one for sorrow. The mice, the hares, the rabbits were invisible in the undergrowth, the foxes were not even properly red, but mud spattered brown, even the robins were elusive and solitary. The pheasants and partridges appeared dressed for a quiet walk in the woods. The whole of nature merged into one tasteful tweed of beige and brown and green.

Why hasn't John taken her to live back in Maine with its definite colours and defined seasons and directness? Perhaps there she would have come out of her shell and at his death exposed her pain rather than repeating 'I'm fine, life goes on' as if life meant anything now. She had loved his Maine with its proper snow. Even the animals were more vibrant. The first time she saw red cardinals like rubies in ivory trees, unashamedly loud and bright and confident, like John had been, she had thought she was seeing things. But he preferred mousy old England.

Dan texted and rang throughout the days. He tried to track her on the map, work out where she'd be at any given time. Waited till she checked in at her B&Bs. She wished he'd leave her alone. The miserable rain soaked into her, running like tears down her dry face. She yelled into the wind when it rose, 'how dare you leave me!' But the anger felt staged, as if she was a bad actress who couldn't unlock the emotion in her heart. She wondered if she could just melt into the mud and dull gorse and defiant trees. Beyond civilisation, she embraced the loss of mobile signal and walked more slowly as the fog rose up from the sea and ice crunched in the grass under her feet.

Beth waited for the fog to steer her over the cliffs, but it didn't. As it cleared, she found herself in a meadow, further inland than she'd thought, nearing a chapel with a large house a little beyond. The light was falling rapidly and under her feet, the ground was like iron. The wet had penetrated her clothes but her shivering had slowed. The ground was like iron and snow was starting to fall. Wet, useless southern English snow. You couldn't ski on it or build igloos with it, but it stopped trains and soaked you.

Struggling to see, Beth made her way to the chapel. She stepped just inside the threshold and looked up to the open sky. It was a ruin. But it was a little out of the wind. Perhaps she'd sit here for a bit. Perhaps she'd lie down for a bit. Above her a little of the light reflecting off snowflakes glimmered and she made out the simple belfry which had a bell suspended in it. How ridiculous. A shiny bell in a ruined belfry. Looking out through the doorway, Beth saw a flock of cardinals clustered round a tree. How amazing! Their colours were so bright in the gloom. But then it was impossible for them to be here. It had to be John's doing. John had come for her but he couldn't find her. She reached for the bell-rope and pulled. A single note echoed out into the twilight. The cardinals flickered. Beth sat on the stone step against the doors down closed her eyes. She was starting to feel warm. John was coming for her and all she had to do was wait.

*****

'We were having a dress rehearsal at the old chapel; we're putting on a medieval concert. Well that's the plan. We'd put the bell in just to create atmosphere. The choir were a bit late, they were getting a bit bogged down in the slush when they heard it. Just as well, they were about to give up and turn back. We found your number in her phone, luckily she'd put you down as emergency contact two. The first didn't answer... oh, I see, I'm so sorry to hear that ... We've got the doctor here with her now. He says not to worry. She'll be fine till you get here. He thinks she'll come round soon. You can't miss the house. It's a way down the lane, but there's an old tree outside covered in red Christmas lights.'

*****

After a while Beth opened her eyes. She didn't know how long a while it had been or even if she'd been asleep or just deep in thought or just blinking. For a few seconds she knew neither what nor who she was. There was just a consciousness of sight without understanding what was seen.

Shortly she realised she was looking at a ceiling and then remembered what a ceiling was. It had a colour which was both dull and suffocating but she couldn't recall its name. Another second passed. Blue. It was a cold blue.

She couldn't remember her own name still but bit by bit her body returned to life. She could feel the pillow beneath her head, the warmth of her mouth, the slow beat of her heart, the rise and fall of her chest, the emptiness of her stomach, the weight of her arms and legs, the impossibly distant fingers and toes flexed and still. She knew she could move if she chose but did not choose. Her mind issued no instructions except to the lungs and heart.

She didn't want to move out of this limbo state; suspended between awareness and mystery. In the end though, she turned her head.

There was a window. A big cold, window with metal frames. Beyond the glass was a garden or a field or grounds and they were filled with fog. Barely visible a huge tree stood as if it watched her from outside. She was good at trees but she could not remember its name. Slowly other senses came back - her mouth tasted of metal and slightly acid. She licked her lips which were dry. She could hear footsteps approaching on an uncarpeted floor and someone speaking, very low, she could sense something inde-scribable: unpleasantness, misery, fear.

But for now she lay, blinkering her mind, looking out at the big tree. Red lights, festooning its bare branches, twinkled through the drifting fog and they reminded her of something. Or someone. And that knowledge warmed her a little.

Deep inside she felt an absence, an abyss - not physical but worse. In a while it would come clear to her. She would remember what she had lost, who she was, where she was. She could not think why, but she knew she was looking forward to the return of pain.

That it meant she was coming back to life.

Candle

Mr Makepeace struggled to remember the last time he'd had a sleepless night. His conscience was clear. Every morning, save Sunday, he got up and went to work where he ran an ethical business with a contented workforce.

Every night, he knelt beside his wife at the bedside and said his prayers. Afterwards, he held her plump body in his plump arms and slept the sleep of the kind at heart. Sometimes his prayers were more fervent as he considered the poor; sometimes they were angry. He wished someone would change the outlook of that parsimonious beast who owned the counting house opposite, whose wretched underpaid clerks toiled on ancient desks with barely a candle between them, scratching away till late in the evening, six days a week. If their miserly employer had been allowed, he would have had them working on Sundays too. He had already decreed that they should come in tomorrow, Christmas Day, while their families sat at home with barely enough money to scrape together a bone for a Christmas feast. The chief clerk had a poorly child too, probably a few good meals away from survival in these cold cruel months. But what could be done? It wasn't for the want of telling. The old curmudgeon was not so much unkind as uncomprehending. Living the life of a pauper, he barely lit a candle or a fire; wearing clothes which had not been in fashion since his youth when powdered wigs were still in style. How could he imagine the needs of the family men who worked for him, eking out their paltry pay to cover rent and food and clothes?

'They needn't have so many children,' the wretch had been heard to argue, as if there was a choice.

Mr Makepeace sighed. He ran his hand over the dome of his stomach and considered whether he was hungry, remembering the emergency stash of sausages on the nightstand. No, it wasn't that. Perhaps reading for a while would send him off again.

With an effort, he extracted his other arm from under Mrs Makepeace and got up, stepping through the bed curtains into the chill of the room. There was still a low glow from the fire and Mr Makepeace, donning a robe over his nightshirt and pushing his feet into slippers, shuffled over to pick up a poker and stir the embers. As he bent to apply a spill to the feeble flame so that he could light a candle, he saw, out of the corner of his eye, a small, plump, startled man sitting in the winged chair. The stranger was glowing and transparent. You could just make out the paisley pattern on the shawl against which he sat.

Mr Makepeace was so surprised, he could think of nothing to say save, 'I didn't know we had a ghost.'

'I'm not a ghost,' the other replied, 'I'm the spirit of Hope and Contentment. I wasn't expecting you to stir. You don't usually.'

Mr Makepeace lit the candle and sat down in the other chair. The draught curled round his ankles and he bent forward to put a log on the fire while keeping his eye on the spirit.

'Should I be afraid?' he asked.

'Not at all. I'm a kind of reflection of you. I wouldn't normally manifest myself, but I've got friends coming over and thought you'd sleep through it.'

Mr Makepeace wasn't sure which question to start with but had opened his mouth anyway, when a vibration in the air made him peer round the wing of the chair to look at the window. The heavy curtains had parted and a slight glow came from outside. The light seemed to be moving and Mr Makepeace, with a puzzled glance at his visitor, got up and padded over to peer through the glass. Outside, snow was falling, flakes coming grey from the sky, turned into diamonds as they tumbled past the sparse street lamps and then resuming their greyness, floated down to drifts below. Mr Makepeace, sighing for the poor, huddled not so far away, was about to close the curtains again when he noticed a light in the bedroom across the road. It was the miser's house. This was someone who barely used candles in the normal course of events, but at midnight? He was peering in astonishment when he saw smoke eke out of the opposite window and shoot across the street to pour through his own window and reconstitute itself in front of him.

It was hard to establish exactly what it was. In one moment, Mr Makepeace perceived a transparent old man, and in another, a transparent child, the two images flip-flopping incessantly. He began to wonder if he should give up eating cheese before bed.

'Taking him back in time took longer than I thought,' said the incomer, sitting down in Mr Makepeace's chair and addressing the other spirit. 'It was hard to get him to stop staring at his lost love. Shame he didn't spend as much time staring at her instead of money back then when he had the chance.'

'I hope this all works,' said the existing spectre, 'has the next shift started?'

The shape-shifter drew a timepiece out of its waistcoat and peered at it, 'any…. minute… now!'

'By the way,' Hope and Contentment added, 'we've got an observer. Not sure how it happened but you're in his chair.'

'Sit ye down,' said the newcomer, getting up and gesturing for Mr Makepeace to reseat himself, 'I'm Past. I do beg your pardon. I expect you wonder what's going on.'

'Well…'

'By the way, Past,' interrupted Hope and Contentment, 'can you turn off that infernal switch? You're giving me a headache.'

Past apologised and his form settled into that of a rather wispy and old-fashioned man, rather similar to Mr Makepeace's neighbour.

'You see, it's like this,' Hope and Contentment started but Past had rushed back over to the window. The others stood round him and peered across the street where, to Mr Makepeace's astonishment, the miser appeared to fly from his window under the armpit of an enormous man in a huge green coat.

'We're trying to teach him to change his ways,' finished Past.

'Are you, er, going to teach me the same thing?' Mr Makepeace asked, a tremor in his voice. He was not terribly fond of heights.

'You don't need it dear sir,' Hope and Contentment answered.

'This one'll take half an hour, I reckon,' said Past, looking at his timepiece again, 'it'll seem longer to the old codfish, but it's like dreams you see, it feels like a lifetime's passed but you've been asleep for no longer than ten minutes. Do you find that Mr M?'

'Er, I'm not much of a dreamer. Usually.'

'Pity. Dreams can be very entertaining. Sometime in the future I expect someone will decide they all mean something. We'll have to ask later.'

'Ask who?'

'You'll see.'

Mr Makepeace lit a pipe. There weren't many times when he wasn't sure what to do, but this was one of them. The two spectres gossiped about hauntings and he decided to sit back and enjoy it. If you're going to dream, you might as well make the most of it.

After a while, they saw the neighbour being bundled back into his bedroom through the unopened glass and shortly afterwards there was another whoosh through the window and a third spirit recomposed himself in front of Mr Makepeace. It was the man in the green coat, looking rather the worse for wear and a little scrawny. Two small children peered out from under the coat. One was clearly starving and the other bored. Mr Makepeace finally felt there was something he could do. Uncovering the plate of sausages on the nightstand, he handed this down and followed it up with the illustrated almanac from the bookcase. Somewhat startled, the children took the offerings and disappeared under the coat again. The spirit seemed to plump out and become somehow rosier.

'Here's a man with a grasp on the essentials,' he boomed.

'This is Present, this is Mr Makepeace' introduced Hope and Contentment, 'how did it go?'

'Well, do you know, it never ceases to amaze me how a man intelligent enough to make a fortune can be so stupid. He knew nothing about the lives of his staff. Bet you know about yours!' he slapped Mr Makepeace on the shoulder, nearly knocking him over. 'He had no idea about that little boy. Makes you weep. Still, he's softening. Maybe it'll work. You've got to hope haven't you - ha ha - Hope!' he slapped Hope and Contentment on the back too and he shimmered with the vibration.

Mr Makepeace was quite glad of Present, who seemed to be blocking the draught somewhat, but there was barely time to work out a sentence to sum up his questions, when the others all rushed back to the window.

Getting up to follow them, Mr Makepeace noted that Christmas morning was nearly here. There was a brightening of the eastern sky, and lights could be seen in attics and kitchens as servants rose to start their work. As he noticed with astonishment that the candle was still burning in the bedroom opposite (which really did mean that he was dreaming) another spirit appeared in Mr Makepeace's chamber. It was hard to make out what this spirit looked like, cloaked as it was. A finger that looked bony in the extreme, reached up to scratch what was presumably a nose in the depths of the hood.

'Think we've cracked it lads,' came an echoey voice, 'oh sorry, Mr M, didn't know you were awake.'

'This is Future,' explained Hope and Contentment, 'Or at least that's his nickname, 'Yet to Come' is a bit longwinded among friends.'

'Here, Future,' boomed Present, 'what did you show him in the end?'

'His gravestone. I showed him that one day, he'll be dead.'

'Well, that's hardly a surprise,' put in Mr Makepeace, finding his voice at last, 'did he think he'd go on forever? It comes to us all.'

'You'd truly be surprised what people think.' echoed Future's voice.

'And besides,' Mr Makepeace went on, 'he's living on scraps and being miserable when he could be enjoying what he's got and sharing it out and being the best he could be.'

The four spectres looked at each other and shrugged. 'Told you he'd never need a lesson,' said Hope and Contentment, 'but I really think we ought to get him back to sleep somehow.'

Mr Makepeace woke to the sound of the curtains been pulled back on the bed and the maid bringing a hot cup of tea. He was still in the armchair but his wife arose and, picking up the almanac from the floor and considering the empty sausage plate, waved her plump finger at him in mock disapproval.

'Here ma'am, come and look at this!' said the maid. Mr and Mrs Makepeace went over to look through the window and saw a small boy making a tall thin snowman outside their neighbour's house. It was clearly meant to represent the miser, down to a scowling stick mouth and hunched shoulders. All of a sudden the bedroom window opposite flew up and the old penny-pincher himself stuck his head out and yelled: 'You! Boy!'. The child cringed back and braced to run as a money bag flew out of the window and nearly struck him on the head.

'Take this, buy the biggest turkey in the butcher's and take it round to my chief clerk's house!'

The boy picked up the bag and stood there, weighing it in his hands.

'And when you come back to tell me you've done it AND that you've been round my employees houses and told them to take a holiday today, a paid holiday, then there will be a reward for you too. Go that?'

The lad nodded and shot off, knocking over the snowman in the process.

'Am I still dreaming?' said Mr Makepeace.

'Only if we are too,' said the maid as she watched the boy barrelling round the corner to the butcher.

'You look peaky, dear,' Mrs Makepeace fussed, tucking the blanket round her husband. 'Perhaps an early Christmas present will reinvigorate you.'

She placed a box on his chest and he opened it with pudgy fingers and smiled. It had been a very strange few hours, but at least here was something to bring him back to earth.

He kissed his wife fondly 'Ah, humbugs,' he said.

'Here, Bertram," asked Mrs Makepeace, poking about on the mantelpiece, 'where's that picture on the bit of cardboard I put up here? You know the one with the snowy scene and people looking merry?'

Mr Makepeace, crunching on candy, looked up and frowned, 'I used it to light my pipe,' he said, 'it was a nice picture, but what was it for?'

'It was from Bill. He painted it especially. It's a new-fangled thing called a Christmas card. I was wondering if we should get Martha to paint one to send back.'

'But everyone knows it's Christmas, we don't need a card to tell us.' Mr Makepeace stretched and started to rise, 'never mind, dear, it'll never catch on.'

Stocking

My littlest brother Joe doesn't remember Mummy. My middle brother Ben thinks he does, but I'm not sure he *really* does. But I remember her. She was good at making things. She made my costume for the Nativity when I was in Reception. I think of her watching me from the audience; I was so proud because I had the best costume ever.

That was three years ago. She never got to see my next play. She never got to see Ben start school. Didn't really get to see Joe at all I think.

Daddy isn't any good at making things. He does try. Mummy used to say he was impatient. 'For goodness sake, Pete' she'd say, 'calm down.' I used to think that 'for goodness sake' was his first name.

One year, me and Ben had to be a camel at the school play and they put Joe on top as one of the Kings. Daddy was supposed to make a costume. It was terrible but Daddy wrote a poem for us to read out. Mrs Williamson didn't want us to read it but all the other kids and the teachers thought it was great. Anyway, here's the poem:

> *It's really hard being a camel,*
> *Everyone says you're a grump,*
> *But I'd like to see **them** being cheerful*
> *Carrying this great awkward hump.*

> *It's really hard being a camel,*
> *You've got to walk such a long way,*
> *And after you've travelled for millions of miles*
> *All they can give you is hay.*

> *It's really hard being a camel,*
> *They load you with bundles and sacks,*
> *You slog through the sun to goodness knows where*

And then you turn round to go back.

It's really hard being a camel,
Carrying incense and gold and such things,
But we get shoved out when they take off the load
And the praises go straight to the kings.

It's really hard being a camel,
But I really don't think that I'd mind,
Except that I'm in a Nativity play
In fact I'm the camel's behind.

The front half can see where he's going,
He's covered in harness and bells,
All I've got going is the hump and a tail
And some very mysterious smells.

Afterwards someone said it brought the house down. I don't know what that means exactly, because the house is still here

We don't have all the stuff the other kids have because Daddy has to spend a lot on the childminder. He explained that to me when I asked why. He always tries to explain, even the hard stuff.

He's good at jokes and at reading stories and doing all the voices. Sometimes he plays music really loud and we all jump about until Mr Jones next door bangs on the wall. Daddy says not to worry because it's good to get things out of our systems and Mr Jones would be happier if he joined in.

Every Christmas he lets us decorate the tree. It's always a bit wonky.

'Mummy would despair,' he says.

Every Christmas Eve we put our stockings up and in the morning we have lovely presents in them. We open them before breakfast and have the tree presents later. When Mummy was alive she had a stocking and so did Daddy, but now Daddy doesn't have one.

So this year we talked it over, me, Ben and Joe.

We put our thinking caps on and found one of Daddy's old socks in the odd sock pile (there are always plenty) and we worked out what to put inside.

There's always something fun. So Ben wrote down every joke he could think of in his best writing on a nice piece of paper. There's always something to learn, so Joe gave him his big toddler building blocks because we thought maybe if Daddy started with the easy stuff he'd get better at playing with the little ones with us. There's always something special. So I talked to our childminder and with her help I sewed a tiny bear out of felt. It looks a bit strange but you can sort of tell what it is and now Daddy has something to cuddle at night. And we put everything in the sock.

And we put a tangerine in too, because it's not a Christmas stocking without a tangerine.

On Christmas Day we rushed down to get our stockings and took them up to open them on Daddy's bed and we said 'Look Daddy Look! There's a stocking for you too!'

Daddy always tries to explain, even the hard stuff. But maybe I'll ask another time how grown-ups can laugh and cry at the same time.

Star

How many years had it taken to get here? Trevor started trying to work it out as he sat in front of the mirror removing the make-up.

The lights were necessarily harsh. He watched himself strip off his character, stroke by stroke, revealing the middle-aged face below; its fine lines and wrinkles, the thin set lips, the touch of grey at his temples. Thank God he hadn't started to go bald. So far, he'd kept off the botox, but he wasn't sure how much longer he could go without it; not if he wanted the TV work to keep coming.

His dressing table was littered with cards and flowers. There was a bottle or two of fizz and some top end chocolates. All the cards gushed with good wishes and delight.

He paused, looking at himself - half his face stripped bare, the other still artificially made young and bright - and for the first time wondered if any of those wishes were real or whether they'd been written with bitterness and envy. Trevor picked up one at random and read it. The person who sent it, who on earth was it? Oh yes, that lad he'd been at drama school with. The one who never quite got the best parts because Trevor had them and Trevor had them because... because he was more talented? Or more persuasive? Or had a richer, more influential family?

Trevor finished his make-up removal and took off his stage costume. He despised having a dresser, afraid they might sell surreptitiously taken photographs of his now sagging body to the tabloids. He didn't want to be a laughing stock. His whole career was built on an image of sex appeal and suave sophistication; last thing he needed was his picture with a belly oozing over the waistband of comfortable underwear, his skin discoloured from too much rich living, the bags under his eyes from too many late nights.

He got dressed in his own things, spotting a card from a discarded lover and another from an actress whose career he had somehow managed to halt - he couldn't really remember how or why. And one of the boxes of chocolates... wasn't that from .... actually he couldn't put a face to the name now.

It was Christmas Eve. The next performance wouldn't be for two days and it was time to go home. Trevor put on his coat and opened the door to his dressing room. His door had the biggest star and his stage name in gold lettering underneath. Once, that had thrilled him. Now he expected nothing less. The rest of the cast had gone to a party. Trevor didn't go to the parties anymore, no-one ever seemed to talk to him, not really talk. They either sucked up to him or made meaningless conversation, the sort that couldn't be used against them. There was no-one left in the theatre apart from the cleaning staff. Someone had organised a collection for the cleaners, but Trevor had had nothing in his wallet. The staff ignored him.

Trevor went out of the stage door into the street. In a film, it would have been snowing. In real life, it was just cold and damp. A thin drizzle fell - more like a mist than rain. The sort of stuff that penetrates to your very soul if you get stuck in it too long.

For a while, he stood in the damp alley behind the theatre. A movement out of the corner of his eye: a vagrant huddled in a corner behind the bins, trying to get some shelter from the rain. Trevor tried to ignore him and pondered which way to go. He could go to a bar and see what he could pick up - only he'd tried that on Christmas Eve last year and it had been a disaster. What sort of person doesn't have somewhere better to be than a stranger's bed on Christmas morning? The vagrant shifted on his slab of cardboard. It was an old man. Or at least he looked old. Perhaps he was only Trevor's age, it was impossible to tell. The homeless refuge wasn't very far away, why wasn't he there? Trevor tried to concentrate on his choices. He could go to a bar, he could just go home to two days of eating the best food and drinking the best wine; enjoying the silence and the gleam of the fairy lights on his awards and trophies. Or maybe, just for once, he could forget he was a star and do something no-one would ever know about, never praise him for and for which he needed no special talent.

Trevor stopped pondering and took off his expensive coat. He turned to the dark corner and said 'come on mate - try this on for size - let's get you to the shelter.'

Church

Near darkness. Tiny flickers of light from our candles as we process up the aisle.

'O come, Thou Day-Spring, come and cheer
'Our spirits by Thine advent here
'Disperse the gloomy clouds of night
'And death's dark shadows put to flight.'

As we walk slowly to the rhythm of our unaccompanied singing, our candle flames briefly reflect in the brass fittings, the golden eagle on the lectern, the holly in the floral displays. The ancient stones are cold around us, but we are not cold, even in our thin choir clothes.

We turn, still singing, the candles lighting our faces perhaps, but to us the congregation is nearly invisible. A few worthies are at the front: the ones who like to be seen, the ones with the best clothes, some of whom will later fish for change in the collection. Then they disappear, melt away.

And then I see beyond the candlelight: worshippers, layer after layer of them. A few are in the cathedral tonight but others are from long ago and far ahead; from a time before this place was even built and on into the future.

Not just worshippers on this very spot but from other places, old churches, plain simple chapels, private rooms, hiding places. Real worshippers. Not people going to church because it is the respectable thing to do, regardless of what they really believe deep down. Not people wanting God to pat them on the back or who use God as the excuse for the vile things they do. People simply there because they have faith in the face of an insane world, in the face of the stupidity of man, looking for help with their own weaknesses not looking to criticise others'. People who look for sense in senselessness; melody in discordance. Some rejoicing in the brightness of their life and others hanging desperately onto the edge - squinting into the depths for a glimpse of a tiny flicker of light. People whose faith makes them want to *be* the brightness not the gloom.

Then our song ends and the reader stands at the lectern and reads: 'the light shines in the darkness, and the darkness has not overcome it.'

Christmas Day

Until I was in my early teens, as far as I can remember, Christmas lunch was cooked by my Great Aunt Evelyn and her daughter whom I called Auntie Kate (although she was actually my second cousin, first cousin to my father).

It was a big family affair with me, my little sister, my parents, my paternal grandparents, Great Aunt Evelyn and Great Uncle Alexander, Auntie Kate, her husband and two sons, Auntie Kate's brother Uncle John, his wife (also called Kate, just to confuse matters) and their three children, plus Great Aunt Natalie (one of my grandfather's other sisters) and her great friend known as Aunt Millie (honorary title only - no relation).

Great Aunt Evelyn and Great Uncle Alex had a large beautiful farmhouse which was split in two from side to side. They lived in the front, overlooking the garden with its flowers and apple trees and Auntie Kate and her family lived in the back and ran the farm itself. Great Aunt Evelyn's kitchen was massive, or at least, that's how I remember it from the few occasions I was allowed inside. On Christmas day it was strictly out of bounds. Through the windows you could vaguely see the two ladies through the steam, rushing about performing the secret mysteries which result in a top class meal. The only sound you could hear was Sally the dog who was shut in the kitchen with them and barked herself senseless whenever visitors came. The reason given for her presence in the kitchen was that she didn't like visitors and she was best out of the way.

The front of the house had a large hall and this was pressed into service as a dining room, the normal one being too small for nineteen. After lunch it was laid for afternoon tea and we withdrew into the sitting room for parlour games, carol singing and entertainment. By entertainment, I mean the children were pressed into entertaining the adults.

One year, when I was coming up for twelve and just teetering on the edge of the adolescence, caught between general lack of confidence and overwhelming self-consciousness, I was pressganged into singing 'The Streets of London' solo and unaccompanied, as my grandmother had found out that I'd just done this at the school carol service. Honestly, facing an audience of two hundred parents is nowhere near as terrifying as singing in front of three great aunts (one honorary) who believed that criticism is character building and praise will make you uppity. Shortly afterwards, my cousin Rebecca accompanying herself on a guitar, sang 'The House of the Rising Sun.' There was baffled murmuring after this; the incongruence of a teenage girl singing about gambling and loose women in the setting of a refined English house which looked as if Agatha Christie might pop in for muffins at any moment was perhaps only realised by the generation in between. I suspect the Greats had no real idea what she was singing about. After being depressed by my song of woe and scandalised by Rebecca's song of sin, the adults instructed the younger generation to cheer everyone up by singing actual carols round the piano while my cousin James played for us.

James and I were the same age and we had gravitated through playing with the same toys to chasing each other round the house when we were younger and were now at the trying to be grown up stage. Chasing around had been less hard work and a lot more fun though, right up to the point where I had crashed into the drinks trolley and knocked blackcurrant cordial all over the new pale green carpet. If Great Aunt Evelyn was critical by default, she was positively murderous when faced with a large deep purple stain soaking into eau de nil wool. I had hidden in the downstairs loo for half an hour. It was cold and lonely but preferable to being fed to Sally the dog. Now I was nearly twelve, older and more sophisticated, I just gazed him with admiration as he confidently trickled from 'Hark the Herald' to 'Deck the Halls' and I sang along hoping that my trilling would make everyone realise I was beautiful and talented and not just a bookworm.

I have some of the old photographs of those fantastic Christmas days. Here's one of us children, the year I was nearly twelve. It's in colour. How I loved that dress, how elegant Rebecca looks, was that really how we did our hair?

Here's another of the whole family squeezed round the lunch tables. Here's one from when I was very small: my little sister (the youngest child) puppy-eyed and serious, sitting on our grandmother's knee; me with a terrible haircut cuddled up to my dad, watching him enjoy another helping; my lovely grandfather, raising a toast, and so on and so on - moments in time frozen in black and white.

Funny to think that when I was fifteen, scary, unsentimental Great Aunt Evelyn died suddenly only a few weeks after my grandfather.

The house and the farm were sold a long long time ago. And I have my own family and am building my own traditions. Now that I am a veteran cook of many Christmas lunches myself, I think of Sally the dog, barking away in the kitchen and it suddenly occurs to me that she was probably there as a means to keep people from interfering, which didn't involve swearing or actual assault.

And one day, when I build my dream house, it will be a bit like that farmhouse, with its veranda, its wide windowed sitting room, its huge kitchen and its sunny garden, sometimes dusted with a little snow. And I'll fill it with Christmas.

Author's Note

In December 2015, I set myself a challenge based on the idea of an advent calendar. I wrote what you might find the doors on pieces of paper and put them in a jar. Every day, I pulled one out at random and wrote a story. Some stories came more easily than others and some of the events taking place at the time have found their way into them - Christmas Trees is an example of this. Before publication I removed some of the original stories and merged others. "Holly", "Train Set", "Carol Singers", "Bell" and "Candle" were written to replace them.

With many thanks to Ashley Bailey and Val Portelli, my reviewers, for their input and support. Also many thanks to Sian Preece, whose encouragement made me enter a short story competition in 2015 and take the leap of faith which ended with this book and "Kindling". Also thanks to Nav Logan who borrow some radioactive turkeys and work out what happened to them.

With apologies to William Shakespeare, Agatha Christie and Charles Dickens for playing with some of their characters.

The verse in "Church" is from the carol "Oh come, oh come, Emmanuel" – the version in Hymns Ancient and Modern (1861)

Paula Harmon was born in North London but her father relocated the family every two years until they settled in South Wales when Paula was eight. She graduated from Chichester University before making her home in Gloucestershire and then Dorset where she has lived since 2005. She is a civil servant, married with two children at university.

https://paulaharmondownes.wordpress.com
https://twitter.com/Paula_S_Harmon
https://www.facebook.com/pg/paulaharmonwrites
Books available from: http://viewauthor.at/PHAuthorpage

Murder Britannica

It's AD 190 in Southern Britain. Lucretia won't let her get-rich-quick scheme be undermined by minor things like her husband's death. But a gruesome discovery leads wise-woman Tryssa to start asking awkward questions.

Murder Durnovaria

It's AD 191. Lucretia last saw Durnovaria as a teenager. Now she's back to claim an inheritance. Who could imagine an old ring bought in the forum could bring lead to Tryssa having to help local magistrate Amicus discover who would rather kill than reveal long-buried truths.

The Cluttering Discombobulator

The story of one man's battle against common sense and the family caught up in the chaos around him.

Kindling

Secrets and mysteries, strangers and friends. Stories as varied and changing as British skies.

The Advent Calendar

Christmas without the hype - stories for midwinter.

The Quest

In a parallel universe, dragons are used for fuel and the people who understand them are feared as spies and traitors.

The Seaside Dragon (a book for children)

Laura and Jane expect a weekend break without wifi. They don't expect to have to rescue their parents from terrible danger.

The Case of the Black Tulips (first in the 'Caster & Fleet Mysteries) (with Liz Hedgecock)

When Katherine Demeray opens a letter, little does she imagine it will lead her to join forces with socialite Connie Swift, racing against time to solve mysteries and right wrongs.

Weird and Peculiar Tales (with Val Portelli)

Short stories from this world and beyond.

Made in the USA
Las Vegas, NV
18 November 2020

11109686R00059